Eddi was a job. An assignment...

Doug reminded himself of this fact as his eyes feasted on the way she moved. She was an assignment, yes, but she was also the most fascinating woman he'd ever met.

"Swear you won't leave my side for an instant? Swear it or I won't go," Eddi said. "As long as you're with me, I can do this."

Ignoring the warning in his brain, Doug reached for her hand. He held it tenderly and reveled in the rush of desire that burned through him. "I'll be right there with you every step of the way."

Before he could fathom her intent, she leaned across and kissed his cheek. In that infinitesimal moment before she drew away, it took every ounce of discipline he possessed not to kiss her back. Not to draw her into his arms and kiss her the way she deserved to be kissed...

GUARDING THE HEIRESS
Debra Webb

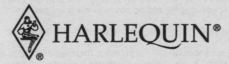

HARLEQUIN®

TORONTO • NEW YORK • LONDON
AMSTERDAM • PARIS • SYDNEY • HAMBURG
STOCKHOLM • ATHENS • TOKYO • MILAN • MADRID
PRAGUE • WARSAW • BUDAPEST • AUCKLAND

This book is dedicated to a bright, beautiful young lady
who never lets anything stop her from reaching her goals.
No matter what life has thrown her way, she always triumphs
while showing kindness and generosity to all those around her.
My niece, Tanya Kimble Turley, this book is for you
and your very own Knight in Shining Armor,
your husband, Ray.

ISBN 0-373-16995-7

GUARDING THE HEIRESS

Copyright © 2003 by Debra Webb.

This edition published by arrangement with Harlequin Books S.A.

Visit us at www.eHarlequin.com

Printed in U.S.A.

ABOUT THE AUTHOR

Debra Webb was born in Scottsboro, Alabama, to parents who taught her that anything is possible if you want it badly enough. She began writing at age nine. Eventually she met and married the man of her dreams and tried some other occupations, including selling vacuum cleaners and working in a factory, a day-care center, a hospital and a department store. When her husband joined the military, they moved to Berlin, Germany, and Debra became a secretary in the commanding general's office. By 1985 they were back in the States, and they finally moved to Tennessee, to a small town where everyone knows everyone else. With the support of her husband and two beautiful daughters, Debra took up writing again, looking to mystery and movies for inspiration. In 1998 her dream of writing for Harlequin came true. You can write to Debra with your comments at P.O. Box 64, Huntland, Tennessee 37345, or visit her Web site at www.DebraWebb.com.

Books by Debra Webb

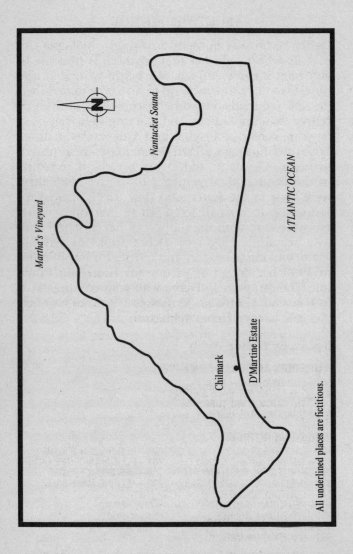

Nantucker Sound

Martha's Vineyard

ATLANTIC OCEAN

Chilmark

D'Martine Estate

All underlined places are fictitious.

Prologue

"Are you sure this young woman is indeed a D'Martine heir?" The man studied him closely, as if he were some kind of bug under a microscope. "I need absolute certainty here. If what you say is true, then—"

"I know what I saw," Joe said sharply. "And I know what it means. I've had twenty long years in the state penitentiary to think about it. That's the only reason I went back there first thing when I got out." He snorted, a disgustingly crude sound judging by the other man's flinch. "You think I bagged that kid twenty-five years ago because I was lucky?"

The other man just stared at him with obvious impatience and no small amount of distaste.

"I bagged him so easy because he was distracted by his girlfriend. He was in love," Joe added with an emphatic wave of his arms. "So damned in love he didn't even notice I was following him until I'd nailed him."

Another flinch from the guy who'd been his partner twenty-five years ago. A partner who hadn't spent a solitary day behind bars and, from the looks of him, had suffered little considering their deal had gone so far south it had burned out somewhere in the vicinity of the equator. Instead of landing a ten-million-dollar ransom as they had planned, they'd ended up with a body to dispose of and nothing to show for their trouble.

He—the silent partner—had insisted they were never to see each other, or even to speak to each other, again. After all, it was his hind end in the sling. The high-and-mighty partner was the mastermind behind the whole plan. Course it wasn't his fault the package had gotten damaged.

Old Joe had no one to blame for that except himself. He'd screwed up. Had too much to drink and the young heir had died as a result, leaving Joe and his partner nothing to do but dump the body and make sure no evidence pointed toward either of them. They'd gotten away with it, by George. Not a soul on earth knew they had been the ones. If Joe hadn't gotten into that other trouble a little later, he'd have walked away clean with a number of crimes to his credit.

But, fact was, he'd spent twenty years in prison. The whole time he'd thought of little else except what he'd missed by screwing up that kidnapping. He could have been drinking tequila down in Cancún; instead, he was wasting away in a cell. Then it had dawned on him that maybe there was hope for a second chance. He'd seen how crazy that rich boy had been over the waitress he'd sneaked away from his hotshot college every weekend to see. A girl like that had no hopes in hell of snagging herself a rich boy without a little leverage, planned or not. Joe had thought on it ever since. The very day the state released him from prison he'd gotten on a bus and headed straight for Meadowbrook, Maryland. He'd hung out for a few days, laying low and acting nonchalant. And, lo and behold, he'd been right.

There was another D'Martine heir. No way could he be wrong. The girl was the spitting image of her daddy. All Joe needed was his old partner to make it happen. To have a second chance at the rest of his life in the land of luxury and pleasure. Damned D'Martines had too much money anyhow. It wouldn't hurt them to share a little. This time he'd make sure nobody got damaged until he had what he wanted.

"All right," his partner finally relented. "I'll set things in motion." He started to turn away, then hesitated. His face turned as hard as the rock wall that surrounded the prison Joe had only recently departed. "But this time there will be no mistakes."

Joe smiled. "No mistakes."

Old Joe might be a little slow, but he never, ever made the same mistake twice.

History was about to repeat itself.

And no one would see it coming.

Chapter One

Doug Cooper waited impatiently in Victoria Colby's office, his anticipation mounting. He'd been stuck on desk duty since taking that bullet six weeks ago. Lucky for him it hadn't hit anything vital, just put him out of commission temporarily.

But now he was ready to get back to work. He was immensely bored with reading reports and studying case scenarios. He was ready for some action. Victoria had briefed him last week on the first case in which he would serve as lead investigator. He wasn't particularly thrilled with the assignment, but he would deal with it. The case, as Victoria had said, was somewhat sensitive and required an investigator with a certain background. Doug understood all that. But that didn't mean he liked it.

He preferred to keep his background exactly there—in the background. He'd worked too hard to put that past behind him. But, as Victoria had said, that very past was pertinent to the case. And Doug wanted his first assignment as a lead investigator. Wanted it badly enough that he was willing to do whatever was required of him. If his roots as the middle son of one of the wealthiest families in America today—one which had been called the last American royal family—would ensure his ability to complete this assignment, he would utilize the highbrow up-bringing and sophisticated education that came with the DNA sequence to which he'd been born.

He thought of the poor unsuspecting female whose life was about to change and felt a twinge of regret. Edwinna Harper had no idea what was about to come her way. Some would say she'd been blessed by fate, but Doug knew better. The gene pool lottery she'd just won carried a high price.

Solange D'Martine was long thought to be the final member of the wealthy D'Martine family line. The last heir to an international jewelry empire that went back for half a dozen generations. Solange, however, was a D'Martine by marriage, not by blood. Still, since there was no one else, she was it. Nearly seventy and agoraphobic, the woman had little in the way of a real life. A nudge of sympathy made Doug sigh. He was certain the lady was lonely. The discovery of an heir would have a dramatic impact on her life. Not to mention it would ensure that the family tradition of designing and trading jewels would, perhaps, carry on despite a tragic past.

Doug had read the file on the devastating events that had befallen the family. The son, Edouard D'Martine, had been the sole heir to the empire, which had its roots in France. During his final year of law school, Edouard had been kidnapped and held for ransom and something had gone terribly wrong. The body was found but the case was never solved. His father had died a short time later from a heart attack, brought on, most believed, by the tragedy. Solange D'Martine had suffered her losses alone. There were some things money simply could not buy and she had learned that the hardest way of all.

Now, a granddaughter, one Edwinna Harper, had been discovered by a close family confidant. The young woman lived in Meadowbrook, Maryland, and worked with her father—or, at least, the man she thought to be her father—in his family-owned hardware store. Edwinna's mother, Millicent, had abruptly married Harvey Harper nearly twenty-six years ago after discovering she was pregnant. Doug wondered why, if in fact Edwinna was Edouard D'Martine's biological child, Millicent hadn't come forward and announced to the world that she carried the child of the recently deceased sole heir to such a massive fortune. Proving paternity, even twenty-five years ago, wasn't that difficult. But Millicent, better known as Milly, had remained oddly silent.

"Sorry to keep you waiting, Douglas," Victoria said as she entered the large office that overlooked the heart of Chicago from the fourth floor of the twenty-story skyscraper that sat only two blocks from the Magnificent Mile. At this hour of the morning shoppers would already be milling about the sidewalks, rushing from one prestigious department store to the next. As she settled behind her wide, polished oak desk, Victoria continued, "I received a call this morning from the D'Martine attorney, Mr. Thurston. Mrs. D'Martine would like us to proceed immediately."

Doug nodded. "I'm ready. I can leave this afternoon."

"Fine. You should arrange a rendezvous time with Mr. Thurston." Victoria studied Doug a moment before adding, "I know that the threat to Miss Harper is only theory, but I want you to approach this assignment as if it were fact."

"Of course."

Something changed in Victoria Colby's eyes then. He'd seen it before anytime the case of a missing child came up. "It would be impossible to properly communicate the depth of pain involved with the loss of a child." She swallowed with difficulty and moistened her lips. "I can fully understand Mrs. D'Martine's desire to be particularly cautious. This young woman is all that remains of her son. Whatever is required for you to protect Miss Harper from harm and to prepare her for the change that is about to take place in her life, you will have this agency's full support. Don't hesitate to follow your instincts. Whatever is necessary."

Doug nodded again. "Rest assured. I won't disappoint Mrs. D'Martine or this agency."

Victoria's somber expression relaxed into a smile. "I'm quite certain you won't disappoint us."

After discussing a few additional minor details, Doug took his leave. A final arrangement or two remained unsettled, such as packing for an indefinite stay in Meadowbrook, Maryland. But only one thing actually concerned him, the ability to keep his true identity secret. If the media got wind of the D'Martine story, especially the tabloids, they would be on it like starving predators going in for the kill. Keeping his face out of the limelight might just prove impossible. His jaw clenched automatically. Somehow he had to do it. Though Doug loved his family, he had no intention of going back to that life. His family might not understand his decision but they respected it. The media, however, respected very little when it came to a hot story.

Edwinna Harper, known to her friends as Eddi, wasn't the only one in danger of losing control of her life here.

Douglas Jamison Cooper-Smith, aka Doug Cooper, had a few secrets of his own.

"I'LL SEE YOUR TEN and raise you twenty."

Eddi Harper paused, wrench midturn, and eyed the card-playing foursome from her position beneath the kitchen sink. This friendly little game of poker had just gotten serious. Ms. Minnie never, ever bet more than ten dollars. A fat droplet of water from the leaking s-trap hit Eddi smack in the middle of her forehead and reminded her of what she was supposed to be doing. She swiped her forehead with her sleeve, then quickly gave the ring another turn, her gaze still glued to the elderly ladies seated around the antique dining table belonging to Ms. Ella Brown.

Mattie Caruthers, Minnie's fraternal twin, raised a speculative eyebrow at her sister. "Call," she stated crossly as she slapped her wager down.

"Now, Mattie, no need to get your knickers in a wad," Ella scolded teasingly before placing her own twenty atop the others. "Adventure is good for the soul."

Irene Marlowe looked up from her splay of cards and smiled at her friends, then placed her bill in the growing pot. "Before we reveal what we're holding," she began in that lusty voice that had once made her a small fortune on the silver screen, "we have another matter to discuss." Irene flicked an assessing glance in Eddi's direction.

Eddi frowned. She twisted the ring one final turn, visually checked her work, then scooted from under the sink. After reaching up and turning on the faucet, she squatted between the open cabinet doors and watched the s-trap for any leaks while the water flowed through the newly installed pipes. She kept a careful watch on the ladies from the corner of her eye. Eddi had a feeling that she was about to hear the down and dirty on some poor unsuspecting Meadowbrook citizen.

"You all may have forgotten, but at the end of this month our Eddi turns twenty-five," Irene reminded. Three properly horrified gazes flitted to Eddi then back to Irene.

Eddi cringed inwardly as she got to her feet. So, she was the poor unsuspecting citizen. Ms. Irene made it sound as if she had developed some terminal illness rather than simply having grown another year older. "All done here, Ms. Ella," Eddi announced as if neither she nor her birthday had been mentioned. Maybe she could derail wherever this was going. And maybe the tooth fairy was real.

"Put it on my account at the hardware," Ella told her quickly, not wanting to spare too much attention from the discussion that was no doubt about to blossom.

"This is not good," Minnie said knowingly. She shook her head slowly from side to side. "Not good at all."

"We have to do something," Mattie chimed in. "Before it's too late."

Too late? Eddi made a face as she rounded up her tools. Sure, she didn't have a romantic prospect in sight, but she hadn't really looked. Who had the time? And it wasn't as if Meadowbrook was brimming with young, single males. But "too late" somehow sounded like a bit of overkill.

Ella took a long, thoughtful draw from her illegally imported Cuban cigar, then tilted her head and blew out the resulting smoke. "You're right," she offered finally. "We have to do something, otherwise our Eddi is doomed."

Eddi glared at the foursome and opened her mouth to argue, but Minnie spoke before she could. "Here, Ella, dear, have some more Remedy." Minnie freshened Ella's iced tea by adding a little of what Eddi knew to be moonshine from the mason jar sitting next to the tea pitcher.

"Thank you." Ella took a hearty swallow and gingerly patted her ample bosom. She sighed. "That's just what I needed."

"The way I see it," Irene said, garnering the group's attention once more, "a prime opportunity has fallen into our laps."

"Oh, do tell," Mattie crooned.

Eddi looked from one blue-haired lady to the next, then shrugged and turned to finish packing up her tools. It was useless to try to stop them. This wouldn't be the first time, or the last, Eddi would bet, that her marital status, or lack thereof, would be discussed by Meadowbrook's most respected matriarchs. The women loved playing Cupid.

"What opportunity?" Minnie asked eagerly of Irene's enigmatic announcement.

"I saw a very handsome young man checking into Ms. Ada's boardinghouse this morning," Irene explained with a dreamy look on her well-preserved face. "He reminded me instantly of JFK Jr. Devilishly handsome, I tell you. My heart hasn't reacted like that since my first on-screen kiss."

Eddi stilled, her fingers on the latches of her bright red toolbox. In a small town like this no stranger went unnoticed. Eddi'd seen the guy. He was the kind of man who inspired phrases like drop-dead gorgeous. At just over six feet, she estimated, and one hundred seventy pounds, the man appeared lean and solid. Not that she made it a habit of sizing up men, especially strangers, but there was just something about this one that aroused her natural curiosity. Thick, dark hair and piercing blue eyes adorned a face that was chiseled to sinfully handsome proportions.

Eddi blinked away the image. The man had rolled into town in his black SUV at nine this morning, all mysterious and good-looking, and, she glanced at her wristwatch, at only two-fifteen, the Club was already talking about him. She glanced at the members in question. No one knew exactly what this "club" did. It was anyone's guess. However, their matchmaking was legendary in these parts. She doubted a soul in town knew what the subject of their discussion did for a living or where he'd come from as of yet, and still she'd bet *they* had already reached a number of conclusions.

But, Eddi admitted as she chewed her lower lip, there was something that bothered her about the man.

It wasn't anything in particular. Maybe something about the way he carried himself. Though she was far from world wise, the one word that came to mind was *dangerous*. The man was like no other she had ever seen, in real life anyway. And Eddi had every intention of giving him a wide berth if their paths crossed. Assuming he stayed in town longer than the night.

"Oh, I saw him, too," Mattie and Minnie chimed simultaneously. Ella nodded, "So did I."

For goodness' sake. Eddi suppressed the urge to heave a sigh and shake her head. Did these ladies do nothing but peek out their windows all day long? Well, she amended, when they weren't playing cards and sipping Remedy. She felt immediately contrite. The elderly foursome was harmless and well-meaning. She should just cut them some slack.

"The only two bachelors the right age left in Meadowbrook think of Eddi as just another one of the boys," Irene was saying with all the drama she had honed over the past half century as an actress. "We certainly can't match her up with either of them, and frankly, ladies, our time is running out."

Eddi snapped shut the latches on her toolbox and pushed to her feet. "Ms. Irene, I appreciate your concern," she began, "but I—"

"But what do we know about the gentleman?" Mattie interjected, cutting Eddi off. "He could be a drifter." Her expression sparkled with renewed interest. "Or…a spy."

Ella rolled her eyes and demanded, "What's to know?" She took another drag from her cigar. "No wedding ring, so he's single. Handsome as they come.

And Ada said he used one of those credit cards that have no spending limit. He's probably loaded."

Eddi's mouth dropped open in disbelief. No ring didn't mean anything and a high credit line certainly didn't equate to wealth. These ladies were shameless! Their conclusions were foolish and unfounded. And they thought Eddi was naive. Enough was enough. "Ms. Ella, I—"

"Run along now, Eddi," Ella scolded gently. "We'll take care of this little problem for you."

"He could be an ax murderer for all we know," Minnie countered suddenly, as if the idea had only just occurred to her. "He had that…that look, you know."

Mattie pooh-poohed her sister's suggestion. "What would an ax murderer be doing in Meadowbrook?" She glared at Minnie. "That look you're referring to is intrigue. The man's a regular Pierce Brosnan."

"Ladies," Eddi said more firmly. She set her hands on her hips and strode to the dining table so that she could glare down at the meddling old biddies more effectively. "I'm not looking for a husband."

Ella tipped her cigar ashes into a nearby ashtray. "It's the curse," she announced solemnly.

Confusion swiftly replaced Eddi's irritation. "Curse?" A bad feeling edged into the back of her mind.

Minnie nodded gravely and looked from one to the other until her gaze came to rest steadily on Eddi. "It's affected the Harper women, as well as the Talkingtons on your momma's side, for generations."

"Every female who didn't marry by the age of twenty-five, *never* married," Ella explained. "Your aunt Jess, your great-aunt Rosie, your cousin Mildred." Ella shrugged. "The list goes on and on. Your momma scarcely made it herself." The four shared another knowing look.

"Come on," Eddi countered. "You don't really believe that stuff." She looked to Irene, usually the most levelheaded one of the matchmaking group. "Those are just coincidences." This was ridiculous. How could they believe this nonsense? It was laughable. Eddi licked her suddenly dry lips.

Almost.

She quickly ran down the history of the named relatives, then considered her own unattached, uninvolved, admittedly romanceless state and dread pooled in her tummy. Maybe they were right. Maybe she was doomed to live a life alone, struggling to keep the hardware from going under.

"Eddi, honey, I'm afraid my friends are right," Irene soothed. "I'm not a suspicious person by nature, but the facts speak for themselves."

Eddi threw up her hands and waved them back and forth as if she could erase the whole subject. "This is the new millennium, ladies, it's okay to be twenty-five and single."

Ella lifted one finely arched gray eyebrow. "But how many twenty-five-year-old virgins do you know?"

The blush started at her toes and rushed all the way to the roots of Eddi's carefully braided hair. "Have a nice afternoon, ladies," she said pointedly. "I think that's my cue to go." Eddi pivoted and strode toward her waiting toolbox.

"Come on, Eddi," Irene cajoled. "It's not your

fault your father had to have your help every spare moment since you turned thirteen. Your mother's accident didn't permit her to provide the extra set of hands he needed. All you've ever known is that hardware store. When other little girls were playing dolls and dress-up, you were learning how to handle a wrench and to swing a hammer. You played baseball and basketball when you were a teenager instead of wearing cheerleader skirts or taking dance lessons.''

Minnie nodded her agreement. ''Your male peers were all too in awe of your athletic ability to ask you for a date.''

Eddi snatched up her toolbox. ''It's not like I've never had a date,'' she snapped.

''Don't get yourself worked up, girlie,'' Mattie put in sternly. ''Everything is going to be just fine.'' She smiled then and winked at Eddi. ''You'll see.''

Eddi blew out a breath of frustration. ''Have a nice day, ladies.'' The well-painted smiles plastered across those sweet, wrinkled faces did nothing to set Eddi at ease as she let herself out the back door. She loaded her toolbox into the back of her pickup truck, dusted her hands on her faded overalls and slid behind the steering wheel. The ancient engine started on the first turn of the key in the ignition. Eddi shifted into reverse and backed up far enough to turn around. She had a full day ahead of her. She didn't have time to waste worrying about husbands or boyfriends, or even dates.

A choked laugh slipped past her lips. So what if she was about to turn twenty-five? There would be plenty of time for her to find a husband and start a family of her own later. With the supercenters located only a few miles away in Aberdeen, keeping the family hardware going was all she could manage, and she accomplished that by the skin of her teeth.

Besides, a good-looking stranger was about as far from husband material, in her opinion, as a member of the male species could get. She knew nothing about the man. So what if he was intriguing? Handsome?

Eddi shivered and pressed harder on the accelerator as she pulled onto the street. She headed toward the town's square and the hardware store. She didn't need a husband. All she needed was the promise of plenty of work to make ends meet the rest of the month.

A little tingle beneath her belly button instantly belied her words.

Eddi stiffened her spine and put a stop to that foolishness. Irene and her buddies were getting to her, that's all. No tall, dark and handsome stranger was going to roll into town and sweep her off her feet. She'd been a good girl her whole life, she wasn't about to start making mistakes now. It didn't take experience in the "sex" department to know that knights in shining armor didn't exist.

She parked in front of the hardware and shut off the truck's engine. The best she could hope for from the handsome stranger was that he'd have some sort of plumbing emergency that required her expertise. With a dry laugh that was a touch too brittle, Eddi strolled through the old-fashioned double doors and into Harper's Hardware, established 1918 by her great-grandfather.

"Hey, Dad." Eddi stepped behind the scarred counter and pressed a kiss to her father's waiting cheek. "Been busy?"

She knew the answer before she asked the question. Small-town hardware stores were nearly a thing of the past. The supercenters had all but put them out of business. But the Harpers hung on, just barely. They weren't going down without a fight. Not as long as Eddi was still breathing.

"'Bout the same as usual," her dad offered his routine reply as he handed her a couple of messages.

Eddi stared at him for a long while before her gaze moved down to the messages in her hand. His gray hair was cut short, his brown eyes more solemn than usual. Her father had always been such a pleasant and jovial man, but when bills piled up, his expression grew more and more grave. She knew he worried, even more so lately. He was worried particularly now. Another three months like the past three and they'd have to consider selling out. She did all she could, just as he did, and most times it managed to be enough. But that little bit of luck had run entirely too thin of late. They'd never make it through the winter if business didn't pick up. There would be no more loans from the bank. Barring a miracle, this time next year…well, she wasn't going to think about that.

She would not give up. Knowing how her father worried always got to her, but she had to be strong. She inhaled a big, bolstering breath. Now was not the time to be a wimp.

She gave her father the brightest smile in her repertoire of masks and produced an optimistic tone. "Well, I've been busy all morning. If this keeps up, by the end of the week we'll be in good shape."

His smile was slow in coming, but it came. "We always get by. Thanks to you."

Eddi quickly shifted her focus to the messages so her father wouldn't see the tears shining in her eyes. They would make it, she would see to it. Mrs. Fairbanks's commode tank probably still wasn't filling properly. Sometimes those fill valves could be a major pain. Eddi shuffled to the next message. Colleen Patterson needed a leak stopped in her bathtub faucet. Eddi could handle those before calling it a day, making today's tally pretty darned good.

She gathered a new fill valve and the seals Mrs. Patterson's faucet most likely needed. Before too long Mrs. Patterson was going to have to surrender to the inevitable and spend the money for a new faucet. Eddi wasn't sure how much longer she could keep that ancient contraption working. But she'd give it her best shot.

"Almost forgot," her dad said abruptly. "Your mom called. She needs you to come by the house before you go anywhere else." He frowned. "She sounded a little odd. Swore there was nothing wrong, but insisted I send you home the next time you stopped in for your messages."

Eddi nodded and beamed another smile. "I'm on my way." She gave her father a little salute and headed for the door. Her forced smile slipped into a frown. Her mother rarely interrupted Eddi's workday. She hoped nothing was wrong. Three days after Eddi's thirteenth birthday her mother had been involved in a horrendous car crash. Though she'd survived, the accident left her with debilitating physical consequences. She could walk with a cane and only short distances at that. Even after dozens of surgeries and years of therapy she couldn't manage any of the housecleaning or cooking that involved more than a minimal amount of walking or standing. She was, however, a woman of perpetual optimism. Eddi scarcely remembered a day in her life that her mother hadn't worn a smile.

Eddi clung to that optimism, made it her own. It was all that got her through the really tough days since she'd learned a long time ago that fairy godmothers didn't exist any more than knights in shining armor did and that all the wishes in the world wouldn't change what was meant to be.

DOUG PRESSED THE DOORBELL a third time and waited for an answer. Next to him on the wide veranda, Mr. Thurston, the D'Martine attorney, adjusted his tie and looked immensely put out by having to wait past the first summons of the home's door chimes.

"I knew we shouldn't have called to warn the woman that we were coming," Thurston muttered. "She's probably made a run for it already."

Choosing to ignore the pretentious attorney, Doug used the time to catalog his surroundings. The Harper home was a small craftsman bungalow with an inviting veranda and a neat, well-kept appearance that made one feel immediately at ease. Well, Doug amended, perhaps anyone but a man like Thurston who likely equated time with money and had already tallied a significant total since leaving Martha's Vineyard.

Like the Harper home, the yard was immaculately maintained. Autumn's first castoffs lay sprinkled about on the lush green grass and bursts of colorful pansies overflowed several pots bordering the four steps that divided the lawn from the veranda.

Finally, the painted door swung inward and a frail woman, wholly dependent upon the cane in her right hand to stay vertical, peered guardedly at them. "Why are you here?"

Millicent Harper. He recognized her from the case files he had reviewed. Her once honey-colored hair was now gray and her brown eyes looked dull with worry as if she expected the worst news. Doug suffered a moment of regret for what he was about to be a party to. But, unfortunately, it was necessary. Edwinna Harper could be in danger when the media discovered her true identity. If someone close to the family had recognized her and rushed to tell Mrs. D'Martine, it was only a matter of time before the right person from the media circus that followed the rich and famous stumbled into Meadowbrook and did the same.

"Mrs. Harper," Thurston said, manufacturing a smile that made his face look as if it were about to crack. He extended one well-manicured hand and added, "I'm Brandon Thurston, attorney for the D'Martine family. My associate, Mr. Cooper—" he gestured vaguely to Doug "—phoned you earlier."

Millicent Harper's demeanor grew even more guarded at the mention of the D'Martine name. She made no move to shake the attorney's outstretched hand. "What do you want?"

"Mr. Cooper is an investigator from Chicago," Thurston said pointedly, leaving out the pertinent details for intimidation purposes. "Mrs. Harper, we'd like to come in. We have a very important matter that should be discussed in private. I think you know the subject.''

She nodded, the gesture seemingly dazed. Doug imagined she felt just that way. A ghost from a twenty-five-year-old past had just invaded her present. It couldn't be a good feeling, especially when she had so obviously built her life well away from that past.

Once they were inside and seated, Doug quickly surveyed the room. Same as the outside, neat, well-maintained, comfortable-looking. Pictures of Edwinna Harper dotted the mantel and walls. The Harpers were clearly proud of their one and only child.

"What is it you want from me?" There was no mistaking the fear in her voice or the wariness.

"Mrs. Harper," Doug said before the mouthpiece next to him on the sofa could screw things up any worse. "We're here about your daughter, Edwinna."

Millicent's eyes widened slightly and her breath caught audibly. "Oh?"

Doug nodded. "Yes, ma'am. We believe Edwinna is the daughter of the late Edouard D'Martine. Can you tell us if that assessment is correct?" Before she could speak, Doug added, "Please be aware that certain steps have already been taken to reach that conclusion." A DNA sample had been taken without Edwinna's knowledge. It was not exactly on the up-and-up, but the deed was done and had been relatively easy to do for whomever the D'Martines had hired for the job. All one needed was a glass the person had used or an envelope with a licked and sealed flap. Hell, even a toothbrush would work just fine. In this case, a soft-drink bottle had been obtained.

Something like defeat stole across Millicent Harper's face. She stared at the floor a moment before meeting Doug's eyes once more. "Before I can tell you anything I have to talk to my daughter first."

"Mrs. Harper," Thurston pressed, "we know all we need to. But, there are things *you* need to know."

She shook her head, tears shining in her eyes. Doug hated himself for being a party to this. They were about to unravel this woman's carefully constructed life. What if her husband didn't know? But, then, how could he not? Doug's gut clenched in sympathy. "We're not here to cause trouble, ma'am," he put in quickly, hoping to allay her fears. "We want to help your daughter."

She held up both hands in a plea for silence. "I have to talk to my daughter first. We can have this discussion later." Her gaze collided with Doug's. "Please."

Doug tried to reassure her with his eyes as he stood. "Of course." He stared down at Thurston and gave him a look that dared him to argue otherwise. "You can find us at the boardinghouse."

Millicent nodded, relief evident in her face. "I'll call you after I've told my daughter."

"Told me what?"

All eyes shifted to the front of the room where Edwinna Harper stood in the doorway.

Edwinna, her expression fiercely guarded, looked from Thurston, who only then pushed to his feet, to Doug and then to her mother. "Who are these people? And what is it you have to tell me?"

Chapter Two

Dead silence filled the room for the space of three beats.

Millicent's gaze swung to Doug's. "Please," she urged.

Knowing full well what she wanted, Doug nodded and offered both Millicent and Edwinna a smile. "You know where to reach us," he reminded the mother. Then he ushered a still-speechless Thurston toward the door. Thurston stalled there, apparently unable to tear his startled gaze from the young woman standing to one side waiting for them to pass.

"My God," Thurston murmured.

"Let's go," Doug insisted, giving Thurston another nudge toward the entry hall. The resemblance between Edwinna and her grandmother D'Martine was uncanny to say the least. But now was not the time to hang around and gawk.

Eddi watched the two strangers exit through the front door with a mixture of anxiety and fear tangling in her belly. Part of it, she confessed, was from the up-close encounter with the gorgeous guy Irene and her pals had gone on so about. The other part, however, was something she couldn't quite label. What were these men talking to her mother about? Her gaze moved back to where her mom still sat in her favorite rocker-recliner, and the knot of anxiety tightened. Milly looked more frightened than Eddi had ever seen her in her entire life.

"What's wrong? What did those men want?" She hurried to her mother's side before she put herself through the physical rigor of getting up. If those guys were bill collectors she was going to teach them a thing or two about manners. The Harpers might be a little late on payments now and then, but they never failed to pay.

Crouching near Milly's chair, she searched those usually smiling brown eyes and found only pain. "Please, Momma, tell me what's happened."

Milly nodded. "I want you to sit down over there." She gestured to the couch. "I have some things to explain to you."

Feeling her own tension heighten, but needing desperately to hear what her mother had to say, Eddi obediently settled on the couch. She wondered briefly how long those men had been here pestering Milly. Then she chastised herself for not coming sooner. If she hadn't piddled so at Ms. Ella's house to listen to the matchmaking plot, she could have been here already.

Milly Harper moistened her lips and blinked away the tears in her eyes. The strength Eddi knew her mother to possess visibly surged and the uncertainty she'd seen moments ago all but vanished.

"There are things I should have told you long ago." She cleared her throat and propped both hands on her cane. "But, selfishly, I chose not to. Now it will be all the more difficult."

Eddi's confusion mounted with each passing second. "What on earth are you talking about?"

Milly took a big breath and began, "Twenty-six years ago I graduated high school and thought I had the world by the tail." She shrugged one shoulder. "My family didn't have any money to speak of, but that wasn't going to stop me. I'd won a scholarship, enough to pay my tuition and such. So, off I went to Boston, to a school I never dreamed I'd have the opportunity to attend. I picked up a waitressing job to keep a little money in my pocket." Her gaze took on a distant look. "I was on my way."

For a long while Milly said nothing else. Eddi knew that she was remembering. She couldn't imagine why she'd never heard this story before. She hadn't even known her mother had attended college, much less some fancy Boston institution.

"I met someone." She fidgeted a bit, the uncertainty creeping back. "He was a little older than me and in his final year of law school." She smiled through the layer of emotion that now shimmered in her eyes. "We fell in love immediately." She shook her head. "It was just like a fairy tale. He was this handsome prince and I was the lowly peasant who'd captured his fancy and his heart."

Eddi was suddenly enthralled by the story, having forgotten all about the strangers she'd found in her own living room. "Mother, you never told me you'd been in love with someone else before Dad."

Milly's eyes met Eddi's briefly. "Well, we all have our secrets."

Another moment of taut silence lapsed between them.

"We had it all planned out. As soon as he graduated we planned to marry." Her gaze flicked to Eddi's. "His parents would never have approved of him marrying a small-town girl like me. But he didn't care. We were in love and that's all that mattered."

The fervor in her mother's voice emphasized the truth in her words. She had been in love with the young man of which she spoke. Deeply in love. Eddi's heart rate picked up its pace in anticipation of more of the story.

"He was about to go home for spring break, his graduation was only weeks away." She smiled sadly. "And we were so happy. I told him then...he was going home to break the news to his parents and then he was coming back for me. He wasn't even going to wait for his graduation...." Her voice trembled then trailed off for a time. When she spoke again, her words were strained. "But he never made it home. Someone, we don't know who since the crime was never solved, kidnapped him...held him for ransom."

"Oh my God." Eddi rushed to her mother's side, crouching next to her and taking her hand in hers in a show of comfort. "That's horrible."

"The ransom was never picked up and no one could understand why, until the...body was found." Her lips trembled and she had to take a second to compose herself. "Whatever went wrong, he wound up dead."

"I'm so sorry, Momma," Eddi soothed. Something niggled at her and she asked, "What did you mean when you said you told him then? Told him what?

What made him decide he wasn't going to wait for graduation to speak to his parents?''

Milly's gaze connected with hers and Eddi knew the truth even before she spoke. ''That I was pregnant with his child…with you. That's why we were so happy.''

Eddi went ice cold then fiery hot. Her head shook of its own volition. She thought of the man she knew as her father…of all that he'd done for her…all that he'd been to her. ''That can't be true. Daddy—''

''Knows the truth,'' Milly put in. ''He knew right up front. But he'd loved me since the third grade. He knew I was in love with Edouard, but he was gone. Your father was willing to play second fiddle if it meant spending the rest of his life with me. He loved me that much. I thank God for him every day. He's all that kept me from losing my mind.''

Eddi managed to make her way to the couch. She wasn't sure she could have stayed upright just then, her legs felt too unsteady. She had to sit down. This was crazy. She was Eddi Harper, daughter of Milly and Harvey Harper. The story she'd just heard simply couldn't be.

Then all the signs hit her at once. The fact that everyone always tried to come up with the name of some Harper ancestor who looked like Eddi. The shock of white hair that started at the center of her forehead and cut a path through her strawberry-blond hair. The fact that her mother had light brown hair and her father had black, well, they were both pretty gray now, but that was beside the point. The brown eyes of her parents when she had blue. Oh, the traits had been blamed on some Harper far in the past, or maybe a Talkington on her mother's side. There was always an excuse.

Now, all that coalesced into an epiphany that pulled the rug a little farther out from under Eddi's feet.

"So, you're saying that this Edouard was really my father and that Dad just kind of stepped in to play the part." She shook her head. "Why didn't you tell me? I'm almost twenty-five years old. Did you think I couldn't handle the truth? Did Daddy worry that I wouldn't love him as much? My God, he's my father. This isn't going to change how I feel about him." She looked straight at her mother then. "Or you."

Tears rolled down Milly's cheeks and Eddi felt immediately contrite for her cross tone. She would have moved back to her mother's side except she still didn't trust her legs to hold her steady.

"I'm sorry, Momma. Please, tell me the rest."

Milly nodded and swiped at her tears. "The reason I didn't tell you or anyone else was because I was afraid."

Eddi frowned. "Afraid of what? That Edouard's parents might give you trouble about custody or something?" That was Eddi's first thought.

Her mother shook her head. "I didn't have time to even think of that." She exhaled a heavy breath. "When Edouard was murdered, I feared for your life as well. You see, Edouard was the one and only heir to huge wealth. With him dead, that left only you. I couldn't risk the same sort of thing happening to you that happened to him."

That reality slammed into Eddi like an unexpected fist to the gut.

"The rich are often targets," her mother went on.

"I didn't want to thrust you in the middle of that kind of danger. I couldn't bear the thought of someone coming after you."

"I have to go." Eddi lunged to her feet with surprising agility. A second ago she wasn't sure she could stand, but now...now the fire of fury burned inside her. This...all of this was uncalled for. She had to stop this runaway train before it became a full-fledged wreck. "I'll be back."

She hurried from the room without looking back. She couldn't bear to see the pain on her mother's face. Milly had been plagued with enough pain in the past. Eddi would allow no one to add to her suffering. She would stop this now.

Three minutes later she parked her truck in front of Ada's Boardinghouse. An old Victorian home that had been in the Garrett family for several generations was well restored and the only thing remotely resembling a bed-and-breakfast in town. Meadowbrook had no hotels. The closest one would be over in Aberdeen. The boardinghouse was really more of a bed-and-breakfast save for two exceptions—Jesse Partin and Mavis Reynolds. The two were permanent residents of the boardinghouse. Had been for nearly half a century. According to Ada, taking in permanent boarders was something the Garretts had done for generations to support the community. Most folks around town were pretty sure Ada just liked the extra cash.

Eddi suddenly stalled halfway to the big old front porch. What if the story about her biological father had already spread around town? If either of the men had told Ada...well, they didn't call her "The Radio" for nothing.

Taking a deep breath for courage, Eddi marched up the steps and across the porch. She didn't hesitate as she entered the front door and smiled as Ada herself looked up from the antique desk stationed in the entry hall that served as the reception area.

"Why, good afternoon, Eddi," Ada crooned. "What brings you here?" Her pleasant smile instantly reversed into a scowl. "Did that confounded Jesse Partin call you about his toilet again? I swear I'm going to boot that man out yet. There's not a blasted thing wrong with that toilet except he doesn't flush it right. Gotta give this old plumbing a little TLC. You said so yourself the last time you were here."

Eddi worked up a smile. "That's right, Ms. Ada. But don't worry, Mr. Partin didn't call. I'm here to see your two out-of-town guests."

One fine white eyebrow winged up her forehead. "You don't say." She studied Eddi with a critical eye for one long moment. "Which one you want to see? The young fella or the one in the fancy suit? I gave them the two best rooms we have. Surely neither of them has a complaint."

Ignoring the ploy for information, Eddi said, "The young one." She had noted a look of sympathy in the younger man's eyes. She couldn't say the same for the older guy. In fact, he gave her the willies.

Ada smiled conspiratorially. "First door on the right."

Eddi nodded her thanks and quickly rounded the newel post to head up the staircase.

"Where's your toolbox?" Ms. Ada asked abruptly.

Eddi stalled, considered her options and told the truth. "I won't need my toolbox for this."

"You tell that big-city fella he's supposed to let me know when something's not working," Ada called after her.

"I sure will," Eddi called back. She planned to tell him a great deal more than that, but Ada didn't need to know.

She wanted him and his hotshot friend out of this town now.

Eddi knocked firmly on the door. She considered how strange fate could be. Only an hour or so ago she was in Ms. Ella's kitchen listening to the matchmakers go on about her nonexistent social life and the handsome stranger in town. Little did she know that this stranger had come here to ruin her *entire* life.

Speak of the devil, he opened the door precisely then. Eddi held her ground, didn't step back as her mind ordered when her gaze settled on the shoulder holster and mean-looking gun he wore. She would tell this guy the way it was and demand that he take his friend and go. Maybe confronting him wasn't smart, especially considering the gun, but she had to do something.

"Miss Harper," he said as if he hadn't expected to see her. He glanced past her, then right and left. "You came alone?"

What'd he expect? A posse? Maybe she should have brought the police chief. Maybe someone official would carry more weight with a guy like this, but she was here now, might as well see her plan through.

"I'd like to talk to you." She waited for him to step aside, but he didn't. He just stared at her, which irritated Eddi all the more. "Privately."

He looked surprised, but quickly recovered. "Of course." He stepped back. "Come in."

Eddi glanced around the room as the door closed behind her. A seating area with a small television was arranged at one end of the room and backlit by two double windows. On the opposite side of the room a queen-size bed flanked by tables and a lovely bureau filled the space. Between a homemade quilt on the bed and lacy curtains on the windows, the place looked downright comfortable with lots of homey touches. The perfect foil for a man who looked every bit the international spy the ladies in the Club had deemed him to be.

"Please have a seat," the man suggested with a wave of his hand toward the overstuffed chairs arranged neatly around a small table.

The bottom abruptly dropped out of Eddi's stomach. Her knees went weak once more. The fire that had sent her barging over here died like the hot coals of a family barbecue beneath an unexpected summer rain.

She sat down with as much decorum as a rock thrown from a mountaintop.

"Would you like me to order something to drink," he offered. "I believe iced tea, lemonade and coffee are on the room-service menu."

She shook her head. Told herself that her sudden loss of fortitude was the unexpected news her mother had broken, but some part of her knew that it was more than that. Yes, she was startled by what her mother had told her and infuriated that this man had come here to upset her life, but there was more. It was him. Something about him put her off balance.

Okay, enough madness, she railed silently. The thought of how much this story getting out would hurt both her father and her mother rekindled the fire that had so suddenly extinguished when she came face-to-face with this enigmatic stranger.

"Who are you?" she demanded. The first sensible thing she'd said since he opened the door.

He sat down adjacent to her, only with a great deal more grace than she had shown. His khaki slacks and blue shirt, even at this hour of the afternoon, looked as fresh and wrinkle free as if they'd just been professionally laundered. Just a hint of shadow darkened his chiseled jaw. And, of course, every perfect hair was in place. All in stark contrast to her plain, slightly disheveled appearance.

"My name is Doug Cooper," he said quietly. His voice was rich and smooth, but laced with sincerity and even what sounded like kindness. "I'm with the Colby Agency, a private investigation agency based in Chicago."

Another jolt of confusion shattered the last of her rational thought. What in the world would a private investigation agency want with her? The answer struck as quickly as the question had. The D'Martines were wealthy. They had obviously hired someone to find her and her mother. At least that explained the gun.

"What do you want?"

The words came out just as emotionlessly as she had intended them. Her whole mind and body felt oddly numb. She wanted to rant and rave…and cry…but the energy to do so was curiously absent.

"Your mother told you about your biological father," he suggested.

She was glad he used the term "biological father" since Harvey Harper was her father, and nothing, certainly not genetics, was going to change that. "Yes."

Mr. Cooper nodded once and actually looked relieved. Eddi didn't even try to figure that one out.

"Then you know that he was the heir to a vast fortune and that his murder remains unsolved."

She had to confess to some regret...sympathy, even, for that tragedy. No one deserved to be murdered. But, other than being the sperm donor and her mother's first love, she still didn't understand what this had to do with her.

"What does this have to do with me, other than the obvious?" she demanded, voicing her thoughts.

Doug studied the woman seated next to him for a time before he answered her question. She had a right to know the whole truth and on her own terms, whether Thurston agreed or not. She was strong, he could see that. She wasn't going to back down until she had the whole story. He respected that.

But, he had a job to do. His first loyalty was to his client. "Solange D'Martine, your paternal grandmother, wants to be a part of your life. You're all that's left of her son."

Fury whipped across that pretty face. "It's a fine time for her to show an interest now," Edwinna snapped. "Where was she when my appendix had to be removed and my father missed three days' work and the medical costs piled up? Or when my mother almost died in an automobile accident?"

Doug understood her anger. She was confused and

hurt, at a number of people. She was doing the only thing she could, lashing out. "Your grandmother just recently learned of your existence."

She made a disgusted sound. "And that's my mother's fault, right? I hope she also knows that my mom was only trying to protect me."

"Mrs. D'Martine, above all others, will understand that," Doug hastened to assure her. "That's why I'm here."

Edwinna narrowed the gaze that looked so damned much like her grandmother D'Martine's. The young woman was in for a hell of a shock. The streak of white hair that highlighted her strawberry blond mane. That penetrating blue gaze. The nose...the chin. Everything. Edwinna Harper was the spitting image of her grandmother and she didn't even know it.

"What do you mean, that's why you're here," she prodded. She was no dummy. She wanted to know the whole deal. Now.

"When your grandmother learned of your existence she immediately feared that if the media found out, they would have a field day. Considering that your father's murder was never solved, she worries that either the original kidnappers or perhaps copycats might try to do the same to you."

Uneasiness slid through Edwinna. Doug watched her posture stiffen and her expression grow more wary. "Why would anyone do that?" Even her tone had grown smaller, more alarmed.

Once the initial shock wore off, she would be far more skeptical, far less receptive to his strategy. He had to somehow make her understand all that could be at stake here, including her life.

"The D'Martine fortune amounts to billions. We're not talking about a paltry sum here. As the heiress to this fortune, your security becomes top priority. There are a lot of people out there who'd like to have a piece of that kind of money. When the word gets out, and trust me, it will, you'll be a walking target."

He'd watched her eyes go wider with each word he'd spoken. Finally, she shook her head and made a face, something between disbelief and consternation.

"Heiress?" She opened her mouth and splayed her hands as if at a loss as to what to say. "I'm no heiress. I'm just a plumber. I don't want to be an heiress. I just want my family to be left alone."

Doug braced his forearms on his widespread knees and leaned a little in her direction. "I'm afraid you don't understand, Miss Harper. It's not a matter of what you want or don't want. You *are* the heiress to the D'Martine jewelry empire. It's your birthright."

Drawing back just in time as she rocketed from her seat, Doug watched her pace the room. He didn't envy her this battle. The whole money thing was enough to contend with, but to suddenly know that your father wasn't your father and that the man who was your father had been murdered…well, it was simply a lot to digest in one sitting.

She stopped abruptly and looked at him. "What about the other man? The suit?"

Doug relaxed a fraction. At least she wasn't going to plunge into denial or run for the door…not yet anyway. "Mr. Thurston. He's the D'Martine family attorney. His job is to inform you of your legal rights and obligations as a member of the D'Martine family."

She looked taken aback. "Obligations? What obligations?"

Doug lifted one shoulder in a noncommittal shrug. "Your grandmother D'Martine wishes to get to know you and to familiarize you with the family business."

She was shaking her head even before he finished. "I already have one family business to take care of. I don't need another."

Doug had had a feeling that this was where the sticking point would be. He pushed to his feet and tucked his hands into his pockets in hopes of keeping things casual, relaxed.

"I understand, as I'm sure Mrs. D'Martine will. However, you should consider long and hard your options. You and your family here would be financially secure for the rest of your lives." He almost laughed at the way he'd automatically minimized the situation. But he needed her cooperative. "The reality is, Miss Harper—"

"Eddi," she corrected.

He nodded once in acknowledgment. "Eddi. Your grandchildren's grandchildren won't even have to worry about money. I'm not sure you quite comprehend the complete picture. When I use the term *heiress,* I use it in its most literal sense. The matter is not something you can simply dismiss."

The vulnerability in those blue eyes tugged at something deep inside him. Made him want to share his own story with her and assure her that he, of all people, understood exactly what she was going through. But he couldn't take that chance. Wouldn't take that chance. He'd worked too hard to separate himself from his past. He couldn't blow it for Eddi Harper, no matter how he wanted to just now. She was strong, self-reliant, she would find her way. His only job was to keep her safe and to give her a few pointers about fitting in along the way.

"I have to talk to my father," she said and turned toward the door. Now she would run...maybe even deny all she'd heard.

"I'll need to go with you," Doug insisted, reaching for his sport jacket.

A frown marred her pretty face when she looked back at him. "I need to do this alone."

He shouldered into his jacket, concealing the gun, which made her feel lots better. "Don't worry, I'll give you plenty of space. But Mrs. D'Martine hired me to keep you safe and I take my work very seriously."

The frown morphed into a look of disbelief. "You're kidding, right?"

"I never kid about my work, Eddi." He moved up next to her at the door. "Until further notice from my employer, I'm your personal bodyguard 24/7."

Eddi sighed loudly, defeatedly. "Ms. Mattie was right," she said wearily. "You are a spy."

Chapter Three

"What is the meaning of this?"

Eddi stared at the lawyer currently blocking her path and wished him away, but it did no good. She glanced at Mr. Cooper as he came up alongside her in the corridor outside his room and prayed he had a plan to get rid of this guy. She wasn't ready to speak to the D'Martine family's legally appointed representative just yet. She had matters to settle with her own family first.

"Where are you going?" Thurston demanded. "Why wasn't I informed that she—" he cut Eddi an annoyed look "—was here?"

Doug held up a hand to quiet him. Thank God, Eddi thought disparagingly. No doubt Ms. Ada was at the bottom of the stairs straining her ears to hear every single word.

"This is not the time or place," Doug said firmly. "We'll be back in a few hours and perhaps Miss Harper will be ready to speak with you then."

"I beg your pardon," Thurston protested, incensed. "As the authorized representative of your employer—"

Doug leaned slightly toward him, which forced him to look down at the man since he was a good two inches taller. "Not...now." He stepped back and motioned for Eddi to precede him to the staircase. "I'll call you as soon as she's ready for a meeting."

Eddi didn't have to look back to know that the lawyer was not a happy camper. A smile lifted the corners of her lips. One prayer answered, she mused. Now, if the good Lord would just help her get through the rest.

"Well, that didn't take very long," Ada said triumphantly as the two descended the stairs. She gifted Mr. Cooper with a suspicious look. "I certainly hope all was in order."

Before Eddi could respond, Mr. Cooper said in a voice silky with charm, "Everything is perfect, Ms. Garrett." He paused at the door where Eddi waited. "Especially since Miss Harper has agreed to have dinner with me."

Ada's eyes immediately bulged and Eddi was sure she saw her ears perk. "Dinner? Oh, my. Well." Her right hand flew to her cheek. "You two have a nice time."

This time Eddi's prayer went unanswered. She'd asked God to let the floor crack open and swallow her up. But it didn't. Instead, Mr. Cooper opened the front door for her like the gentleman he was. She couldn't stop staring at him as they strolled down the sidewalk toward the curb. He looked pleased with himself, as if he'd just managed some coup. She imagined that he believed he'd headed off any gossip related to why he was really here.

The sad thing was he'd done something far worse.

He'd just set Meadowbrook's infamous matchmakers in motion. Eddi could almost hear Ada on the telephone now putting a call through to Ella or Irene or maybe Minnie and Mattie. Eddi looked up at the overhead power and telephone lines strung along the street. News that she had a dinner "date" with the stranger in town was no doubt buzzing along that very line right this moment.

Mr. Cooper paused where the boardinghouse sidewalk intersected the one along the street. "I hope you don't mind my taking that liberty. I felt sure you wanted to keep the real story under wraps for the moment. Feeding Ms. Garrett that misleading information should provide an acceptable cover for our real business here. A distraction, so to speak."

It took every ounce of willpower Eddi possessed not to laugh out loud. She just wagged her head back and forth. "You have no idea."

Doug was still a little confused by Eddi's remark as he pulled up behind her truck in front of the Harper residence. Maybe she didn't approve of his methods. She had called him a spy. It was possible she didn't fully grasp why he was here. Right now she wanted to check on her mother before going to the hardware to speak to her father.

Going to the hardware store wouldn't be necessary, it seemed. Her father sat on the front steps of his home, his head hung between hunched shoulders.

Doug blocked the memory of the hurt he'd seen in Millicent Harper's eyes. Though Doug felt sympathetic toward his employer, this whole affair was going to change so many lives, perhaps do irreversible damage. It was almost heartless, ruthless even.

But the decision had not been his. He watched Eddi take a seat next to her dad on the top stone step. Already Doug had lost his objectivity. Empathized with her far too much…respected her more than he'd anticipated. He couldn't say for sure what he'd expected when he read her profile, but this earnest young woman was not it.

And she was a plumber. A smile tugged the corners of his mouth upward. She wore overalls, for Pete's sake. Overalls and sneakers and a plain old white T-shirt. The long braid of strawberry-blond hair mixed with the blue eyes and scattering of freckles across her pert little nose personified the all-American-girl look. The getup she wore lent a tomboyish quality to the package. But the streak of white hair that blazed a narrow trail from her forehead to the tip of her braid spoke of breeding and elegance. Though Solange D'Martine didn't wear her hair in a braid, she had the same strawberry blond tresses with that shock of sophistication. The perfect balance between the set of her eyes and the tilt of her nose, and those high-boned cheeks were exactly the same.

The father, Edouard, had had the same coloring, only his hair had been slightly darker, redder. The case file contained a picture of the father as well as the grandmother for showing to Eddi when the time was right. There were documents, all of which the attorney kept safely tucked in his leather briefcase.

Doug sighed, tired. He made no move to get out of his vehicle, but watched his principal from there. This carefree young woman had no idea how very much her life was about to change. Nothing would ever be the same again. With the kind of wealth possessed by the D'Martines came a certain level of public scrutiny. There would be no escaping it. Eddi needed to enjoy her final few days of true privacy, because as soon as the media got wind of her existence any real privacy would be a thing of the past.

"ISN'T YOUR FRIEND getting out?" her dad asked.

Eddi shook her head and refrained from correcting her father as to the friend remark. "He said he'd give me some space."

She was really glad Mr. Cooper had stuck by his word. She needed these few moments with her father. Needed to reassure him and herself.

"So Mom's taking this okay," she ventured. When she'd first arrived home and found her father sitting on the front steps she'd almost panicked. The thought that something could have happened to her mother while she was selfishly demanding answers from Mr. Cooper hadn't occurred to her. And it should have. Usually Eddi wasn't as thoughtless as that. But today had been a little extreme all the way around.

"She's okay," her father said quietly. "She's lying down now."

Eddi nodded. "That's good." She bent her knees and clasped her arms around them, then braced her chin there. "You know this is all just absolutely bizarre, don't you?"

Her father nodded. "But it's true. Your mother and I wanted to protect you, but maybe we should have told you a long time ago."

"I don't want to know now," Eddi argued. "Why would I have wanted to know before?"

Her father smiled and her heavy heart lifted just a

little. "Well, now, I don't think I could have put it any better myself. It's a bit of a thorny patch, that's a fact." He rested his gaze on hers. "But we love you. We've always loved you. If we made a mistake, it was in the name of love."

She hugged her father then. Hugged him with all her might. "You didn't make a mistake." She drew back and blinked away the confounded mist that clouded her vision. She didn't want him to see her cry. "Don't ever think it, not for a second. Okay?"

He nodded hesitantly. "But your grandmother Solange could have offered you much more than we have."

Eddi laughed to keep from crying. "Now, what would I do with a jewelry empire? If it won't stop a leak in old Mrs. Fairbanks's toilet, what good is it?"

Her father managed a strained laugh at that. "I guess you have a point there, girlie."

His expression turned somber once more and the silence lengthened. Eddi felt certain that he didn't know where to take the conversation from here any more than she did. What did one say at a time like this?

"You know this isn't going to go away just because you want it to," he said eventually, his tone as grim as she felt at the moment.

She nodded. "I know." She hugged her knees to her chest once more. "What am I supposed to do?"

"Well." Her father scratched his head and considered the question for a time. "It seems to me that you owe it to yourself as well as your grandmother to get to know her."

"I already have the best two grandmothers anyone

could want," Eddi protested. "What do I need with another?"

"Look here, girlie." Her father looped an arm around her slumped shoulders. "You deserve better than to be a plumber the rest of your life." He shushed her with a firm look when she would have rebutted. "Slaving away at that hardware isn't the answer either. I want better for you same as my daddy wanted better for me. We're scarcely hanging on to that old place anyway. It's past time I sold out and retired." He lifted one shoulder and let it fall. "Truth is, I've only hung on so I wouldn't let you down. What do I need with that old place to fool with day in and day out? Your mother and I could take up gardening or some such." He pressed a kiss to her forehead. "Whatever happens, I know you'll do the right thing."

Knots of anxiety tangled in her stomach once more. She knew what he was doing. He wanted to give her an out. Her father loved that old hardware store and she knew it. He'd be lost without it to go to every day. Her mother hated gardening other than a pot or two of flowers. She had preferred knitting or needlepoint over gardening even before her accident.

Out of the blue, inspiration struck. A slow smile slid across Eddi's face. Why hadn't she thought of that already?

Eddi threw her arms around her father and hugged him again. "Dad, you're a genius!" She shot to her feet and beamed a smile down at him. "Tell Mom I won't be by for dinner tonight. I have something to do."

Her father waved a goodbye as she loped out to

Mr. Cooper's SUV. "Are we still on for dinner?" she asked the handsome man watching her so steadily.

"Absolutely." He allowed her one of those smiles that literally oozed with magnetism.

Before she melted right there on the sidewalk, she said, "Follow me to my place. I need to change."

Three traffic lights and five turns later, she pulled into the driveway of her small cottage. The little house had once belonged to her grandmother and grandfather Harper, but since they'd relocated to the retirement home, she'd moved in. She loved the place. Even as a child she'd known that one day she wanted to live here.

The small stone cottage sat amid a cluster of shady trees with only a small patch of grass to mow out front and nothing but flagstone pavers and flower beds out back. Two tiny bedrooms and only one bath, along with a nice-size living-dining room combination and kitchen made up the interior. She even had her own little fireplace.

Exhaling a satisfied sigh at being home at last, Eddi hopped out of her truck and practically skipped up the path that led to her front door. The answer was so simple. Relief was like a soothing balm, she felt immensely better already. Before going inside, she reached in the box hanging by the door and retrieved the day's mail. "Bills, bills, bills," she muttered. Nothing she wanted to see tonight.

"Nice place," Mr. Cooper commented as he moved up behind her.

Despite all that had happened and knowing that he had brought this unsettling news upon her, Eddi shivered at the sound of his voice. As smooth as satin and every bit as rich. She shook off the thought and jammed her key into the lock.

"Thank you. It belongs to my grandparents. They let me use it since they live at the retirement home now."

See, she wanted to add, my family already takes good care of itself. We don't need anything from the D'Martines.

She tucked her key back into her pocket and pushed open the door. Well, that wasn't entirely true. Still, she had to approach this logically. She couldn't let emotions play into it at all. And that would be difficult. She'd always been ruled by her heart ensuring that she'd been faced with *difficult* before. She could handle this.

She flipped on the light and held the door for Mr. Cooper to come on inside. She found herself holding her breath as he passed then stood in the middle of the room and took in the cozy living area. Never once had she imagined how this place would look to a stranger. She'd never had a stranger over before. She tried to see the room from his eyes, with its high ceilings and thick crown moldings. Her grandfather had loved working with his hands and had detailed every square inch of woodwork in this house himself. The floors were hardwood, but thick rugs covered most of it. The furniture was worn comfortable and a vintage she couldn't name...early fifties maybe. An interior designer or decorator she wasn't. But line up faucets in front of her and she could name the year and the manufacturer.

"I'll just be a moment, Mr. Cooper," she said,

breaking into his careful study of her natural habitat. "Make yourself at home."

He turned to her then. "Doug. Please, call me Doug."

She nodded and forced a smile. "Be back in two shakes, Doug."

In her bedroom she closed the door and suddenly wondered what on earth she would wear. Okay, she told herself, it wasn't as if it was a date. She could wear any old thing.

But where would they go?

She mentally ticked off all four of the local restaurants and finally decided on Randy's. The place was the nicest in town and served a wide variety of entrées. Though she didn't expect Mr. Cooper—Doug, she amended—to be impressed, at least he wouldn't go hungry.

Clothes…what to wear? She chewed her lower lip and tried to decide if she even still owned a dress other than the ones she wore to church, which were sorely out of date and totally unflattering. She had gone to her five-year high-school reunion a couple of years ago. Hadn't she bought something then?

Sixty seconds later she'd gone through her entire closet to finally find the dress in question on the last hanger on the opposite side from where she'd started. Just her luck.

The dress was black…that was good. She'd seen ladies wear little black dresses into Randy's. The problem was, it had long sleeves and it was unseasonably warm out tonight and the hem was just a smidgen on the long side with a floppy ruffle. But that had been the style two years ago. Or maybe it was simply the one dress on the clearance rack she'd liked.

Oh, well. It wasn't as though she had a lot of choices.

She couldn't keep her guest waiting forever. With that in mind she rushed through a sponge bath and twisted her hair up into a bun of sorts. No kind of makeup ever looked good with her complexion so she didn't even bother. A spritz of fruit-scented spray and she was ready.

But the dress…well, it looked kind of pitiful. She glanced at the clock on her bedside table and realized twenty minutes had passed. She didn't have time for this…but this was her first *sort of* date in two years. Now that she thought about it, she hadn't been out since her five-year reunion. How pathetic was that? And she remembered well the looks her dress had gotten that night. The best description she could call to mind was pained. Her friends had lied and said she looked great but she hadn't missed the uncomfortable expressions on their faces when they said it. Okay, so the dress sucked in its current state.

She couldn't take those kind of looks to-night…especially not from Doug Cooper, body-guard…spy…or whatever. She'd had too much dumped on her today already. Any more sympathy from the guy and she might just throw up.

Holding her breath, she did the only thing she could. She ripped off the left sleeve. Just tugged it clean loose from the shoulder of the dress and off her arm. She looked at her bare arm and then the covered one. Minus the sleeve was definitely better. With a firm hand she did the same to the right sleeve.

"Not bad," she murmured as she leaned closer to the mirror and picked away the remnants of thread clinging here and there where the sleeves had previously attached. She stood back and looked herself up and down once more. The neckline was a little high, which couldn't be changed, and the dress was still too long. The ruffle had to go.

Eddi reached for the edge of the ruffle and a soft rap echoed at her door. Her breath caught and she almost toppled over.

"Is everything all right?"

She glanced at the clock once more and noted the time. Thirty minutes. No wonder he'd gotten worried. "I'll be right out."

Scarcely breathing, she listened for the telltale footfalls as he moved back to the living room before she snagged the edge of the ruffle. The ruffle didn't want to come off quite so easily. By the time she'd pulled it off all the way around, she'd almost broken a sweat. After picking away the thread remnants, she eyed her reflection one last time. Now the hem of the dress hit just below midthigh. She smiled, pleased with what she had achieved. The dress actually looked like the typical black sheath one would purchase for a cocktail party or any other number of social affairs.

And it hadn't cost her a dime.

Pleased with her ingenuity, she smoothed her hands over the fabric, enjoying the way it clung to her body. Okay. Now she was ready. Shedding a little of her "good girl" image would boost her self-confidence in this stranger's presence. At least she hoped it would.

DOUG HAD SURVEYED every photograph and piece of needlepoint displayed in the quaint living room. He had even scanned the evening paper. By the time Eddi had finally come out of her room, he'd been contemplating turning on the television to catch the evening news.

But, he had to admit, she was indubitably worth the wait.

Never in a million years had he expected the plumber to clean up so well, but she definitely did.

"Sorry to keep you waiting," she offered as she breezed into the room.

The creamy, smooth look of her skin combined with the fiery highlights of her hair and the curve-hugging little black dress was nothing short of inspiring. Unfortunately the thoughts it inspired were way out of line.

"What's wrong?" she teased. "Didn't you expect me to own a dress?"

Not quite that dress, he said to himself before saying to her, "I never underestimate a lady. I'm only surprised that you would bother on my account."

She moved toward the door a little slower than what was normal for her. The shoes, he decided. The heels weren't stilettos, but they were high-heeled when compared to the sneakers she seemed to prefer. Once at the door she turned back to him and smiled, a calculated twist of her lips that fell just shy of seductive. Another surprise. Or maybe she simply didn't realize just how appealing she looked when she tried.

"No bother." She lifted a speculative eyebrow. "Besides, this has certainly been the day for surprises."

Indeed, he mused.

After settling Eddi into the passenger seat of his SUV, Doug moved around to the other side and climbed in. "Where to?"

"A place called Randy's." She quickly spouted off the directions, which weren't complicated since Meadowbrook was a small town.

Within minutes of their arrival at the restaurant they were seated and their orders taken. Doug conceded that the place was better than he'd hoped for. On a Wednesday night the crowd was light, but the atmosphere was pleasant and private.

He waited for her to start firing questions at him but it didn't happen. She seemed content just to sit and enjoy their relaxing surroundings. Maybe she expected him to make the first move.

"Do you have any questions regarding what I've told you so far?"

She studied him for a long moment as if contemplating how to proceed. He couldn't quite read the emotion in her eyes but there was something there. Trepidation perhaps.

"I only have one question," she said, her tone carefully devoid of inflection.

Doug's instincts went on point. "What would that be?"

"What *precisely* is it that Mrs. D'Mar—my grandmother," she amended, "wants from me?"

He inclined his head and quoted the agenda he'd been given. "She wants to be a part of your life. She wants to know you and for you to know the family business."

That blue gaze narrowed slightly. "I don't believe that's all there is to it."

Their server arrived and Doug waited until he'd placed the salads in front of them and hurried away before continuing, "What makes you say that?"

Eddi stared at her salad a moment then shifted that penetrating focus back to him. "That's just too simple. She must want more. Surely she doesn't expect me to actually handle business affairs. The only thing I know about jewelry is that I can't afford any of the good stuff."

Doug leaned back more fully in his chair and considered the lovely woman across the table for a moment before he replied, "A board of directors and a very savvy CEO run the day-to-day business. With that aside, what do you want or expect? It seems to me that you've come to some sort of decision." And he did have that feeling. After she'd spoken to her father she appeared to have reached some conclusion. He felt a certain ease about her that hadn't been there before. That's why she'd agreed to dinner, he surmised.

"I've decided that if, in fact, I am heiress to such a great fortune that the least I can do is help my family." She looked directly at him then. "My *real* family."

Clarification hadn't been necessary. He knew who she meant. "I can't imagine that Mrs. D'Martine would expect otherwise."

"Good, because that's the only way I will get involved is if it helps my family."

Doug figured that was as close to an agreement as they were going to get for the time being.

"You understand that I'll be your constant shadow—day and night—until further notice, and that there are details that must be worked out first."

She looked startled but nodded hesitantly, then ventured, "What sort of details?"

Now came the hard part. "There is no way to protect you from the media frenzy that will no doubt descend the moment the first whiff of this story hits the air. In order to protect the D'Martine interests as well as your own, you need to be prepared for that."

A tiny frown line wiggled its way across her otherwise smooth forehead. "Prepared how?"

"As a member of a family of that social stature, there are certain outward expectations. Along with the title of heiress comes specific public obligations and assumptions."

The frown deepened. "So, you're saying that to help my family I have to dress and act like a D'Martine heiress?"

"Exactly."

She shrugged. "Makes sense but I'm not sure I know how to act like one of *them*. I'm just a regular girl…a *real* person."

To say he was surprised at her willingness to cooperate would have been an enormous understatement. He was surprised and relieved. Enough so he didn't bother explaining that not all wealthy people fell into the category of *them* just as all nonwealthy people weren't *real* as she put it. He'd stopped trying to clarify his position long ago. What she didn't know wouldn't hurt her. "Any other questions?"

She took some time before she answered. He

waited, almost afraid her willingness would suddenly evaporate, then she said, "Just one."

He gestured for her to go on.

"Can you teach me how to act like an heiress?"

"IT'S NOT TOO LATE," his partner argued vehemently.

It sounded a little late to Joe. But he listened to the voice on the other end of the line just the same.

"I put everything on the line twenty-five years ago and you failed. Failure is not acceptable this time. It doesn't matter that a bodyguard is in place already. All we need is the proper distraction."

That was true enough. Joe had watched the last D'Martine he'd had in the crosshairs fall because he'd been distracted. It could work just as well for this one.

"What kind of distraction do we need?" As far as he could tell there was no love interest in the girl's life.

His partner laughed but the sound held no humor. "I think that's been taken care of for us already."

A smile split Joe's beard-stubbled face as he considered what his old friend meant. "Just let me know when you're ready." He hung up without the usual niceties. No point wasting the breath. His relationship with his partner would be over soon enough. Joe had made a few more decisions on his own during the last twenty-four hours.

If they got a shot at this second chance, and it looked as if they might, there were not going to be any mistakes this time.

And this time there wasn't going to be anyone to share the money with when it was finally his.

The D'Martine heir wasn't the only one living on borrowed time. So was his old friend and partner.

Chapter Four

"Be still!"

"How can I be still when my legs are trembling from the strain of holding up your fat—"

"*Mattie,*" Minnie warned. "We're all under pressure here."

Mattie glared at her twin sister, but she was right. If they didn't hold Irene up where she could see, none of them would learn anything about what was going on at Eddi's house. Mattie felt sure she would not live through the day if she didn't find out what that stranger…that spy was doing with poor, sweet little Eddi. It was 9:00 a.m. already and Eddi hadn't left for the hardware and Irene was pretty sure the young man had stayed the night. Mattie shivered at the idea. Not that she blamed Eddi, but the man was a stranger…could be a criminal even. But, oh, what a deliciously handsome one!

Bolstering her strength, Mattie tightened her hold on Irene's left leg. "So, tell us what's going on in there, would you?" she demanded stiffly. "I don't know how much longer I can hold out."

Ella took a long drag from her cigar, then huffed,

"That's all you do is complain, Mattie. I swear I've never known anyone who could complain as much as you."

Mattie lifted a skeptical eyebrow and glared at Ella who remained relaxed against Irene's '54 Cadillac as if it were her personal prop. "I don't see you over here helping out," Mattie snapped.

Ella rolled her eyes so far back in her head she'd surely have gotten a glimpse of her brain if she'd had one. "You know I can't do any lifting with my bad back."

Her own strain showing as she hung on to Irene's other leg, Minnie harrumphed. "We won't go into how you got that bad back."

A victorious smile stretched across Mattie's lips. Way to go, sis, she cheered silently.

Ella looked properly put upon. "Just because I've had seven husbands doesn't mean—"

"Shh," warned Irene. "I can see them now."

Peeking over the row of hedges and using a pair of bird-watching binoculars, Irene leaned forward for a better view through the kitchen window. Mattie and Minnie groaned with the awkward move.

"What do you see?" Mattie hissed. It had better be good considering all this trouble. It was a good thing Mr. Curtis, Eddi's neighbor, wasn't home or he'd have been getting a hell of a view of Irene's considerable tush as she leaned over that privet hedge. Of course, Irene would say that her tush was just right in a Marilyn Monroe sort of way, but Mattie simply called it *fat*.

Minnie blew the tail of Irene's skirt out of her face and demanded, "Tell us something, Irene."

"Both of the strangers are there."

Minnie's eyes went as wide as Mattie's own surely had.

"The older one," Irene went on in a stage whisper, "the one in the designer suit just opened his leather briefcase."

A simultaneous gasp echoed from the threesome on the ground.

"The good-looking young one—the one who looks like JFK Jr.—"

"Pierce Brosnan," Ella argued, cutting Irene off.

"Shut up, Ella," Mattie griped. "We want to know what Irene can see, not what you think."

Ella simply rolled her eyes again and puffed away on her contraband.

"The good-looking one is speaking to her now." A dreamy sigh. "Oh, if you could only see the way our Eddi looks at him. He's the one. I just know it."

"I've only seen him once but he looks like the one to me," Ella said, adding her two cents' worth. Which, in Mattie's estimation, wasn't worth even one cent, and which she promptly proceeded to state out loud for all to hear, "If he's a man and still breathing, you'd think he was the one."

Ella straightened, incredibly without flinching considering her back was so *bad,* marched over and stabbed a long, blood-red nail right in Mattie's face. "Listen here, Miss High-and—"

"Will you two give it a rest?" Minnie ordered. "We've got to think about Eddi right now, not ourselves."

Ella glared silently at Mattie. If Mattie hadn't been holding up Irene's big butt she'd have kicked Ella's right then and there. But Minnie was right. This was about Eddi.

"Okay, okay. Listen up," Irene announced, garnering their full attention. Her tone turned mysterious then, "Eddi has picked up a pen to sign some sort of document."

Another collective gasp.

"She signed it!"

Minnie, Mattie and Ella all looked from one to the other.

"Now the one in the suit is packing up his brief-case," Irene said in a rush, "including the signed document...he's leaving." Irene made a startled sound. "He's going to kiss her!"

"What?" Ella demanded, craning her neck to look up at Irene.

"Who's going to kiss her?" Mattie seconded the demand, wishing she could see for herself what the heck was going on.

"The old one?" Minnie asked with a frown.

"No," Irene growled impatiently, glancing down at them. "The young one." She peered through the binoculars once more. "He—oh...my...God."

Before Mattie could insist on an elaboration, Irene's weight shifted. Minnie gasped. Mattie's grip on Irene's left leg slipped. Minnie lost whatever balance she'd managed to maintain. They all went down in a tangle of arms and legs and rayon, bowling over Ella en route.

"HOLD STILL JUST a second longer," Doug murmured.

Any oxygen Eddi's lungs had contained evaporated

the moment Doug Cooper moved in close. She scolded herself silently for reacting in such a way, but she simply couldn't help herself. He stood so close that she could smell his cologne, something understated and elegant, yet intensely masculine.

How was she supposed to hold still when her whole body was strumming in anticipation of his touch? He tucked the tiny mechanism, no larger than the tip of a pencil eraser, behind her ear and pressed it against the skin there. Her breath caught in spite of her best efforts not to allow him to know how he affected her.

He stepped back and smiled reassuringly. "Now you're officially on the Colby Agency radar screen."

She chewed her lower lip and tried to decide if that was good or not. "So if anyone really does try to kidnap me, you'll know where I am all the time."

He nodded. "That's right. It's our latest technology."

What did she say next? Eddi clasped her hands behind her back and searched for something else to say, finally deciding upon a question she'd already asked. "You're sure that the document I signed doesn't obligate me to anything I'll regret later?"

"Absolutely not. Our agency attorney reviewed the confidentiality agreement. I wouldn't have encouraged you to sign it had there been any question. Mr. Thurston has an excellent reputation but we always double-check everything."

As he spoke, Eddi found herself cataloging the details of her new shadow, Doug. The white shirt looked good against his tanned skin and the navy slacks were neatly pressed and well fitted. The only accessory he wore was a gold watch that looked incredibly expensive. The black loafers were polished to a high shine. Every thick, wavy hair was in place. He stood at least five inches taller than her five-seven and looked to be quite muscular beneath the starched cotton shirt. Since he was trained as a bodyguard, she imagined that he was well versed in self-defense and other necessary skills. And, of course, there was the gun.

Were all his clients women? she wondered. Did all of them get tongue-tied and feel all tingly inside when he was near as she did?

"Don't you agree?"

His question jerked her from her silly musings. "Excuse me?"

The expression of amusement on his face told her unquestionably that he had read her mind, had noted her preoccupation with his numerous physical assets. Heat scalded her cheeks, only making bad matters worse.

"I was saying that it was merely good business practice for any company to require those with intimate knowledge of assets and so forth to sign an agreement stating that the knowledge will be kept confidential and not used for personal gain."

She nodded adamantly. "Sure. I understand. I guess I just hadn't considered that I would be privy to those kinds of intimate details." Eddi retreated a step, hoping he wouldn't notice.

As if suddenly aware of her discomfort, he moved away, taking a seat on the sofa.

Weak with relief, Eddi did the same, only she chose a side chair across the coffee table from him. This was much, much better.

"Now that you've signed the agreement, I can be a bit more frank regarding Mrs. D'Martine's wishes."

Uh-oh. And she'd thought she knew everything going into this. At least the conversation kept her mind off him. Eddi braced for the rest of the story.

"Your grandmother isn't simply looking for an heir on to whom to pass her vast fortune. She's looking for someone who will truly care about what the D'Martine family name really stands for. Their international jewel-trading business has been more than a hundred years and several generations in the making. It's very important to her that this becomes important to you as well."

Eddi threw up her hands. "Wait just a minute. I told you that I already had a business to run and that I wasn't interested in another, no matter how exciting it sounds." She snapped her mouth shut, barely suppressing the urge to slap her hand over it. Darn it. She hadn't intended to say exciting. She didn't want him to know she'd decided the whole thing sounded exceedingly exciting on certain levels. She'd lain in bed last night unable to sleep knowing he was right out here on her sofa. She'd tossed and turned and thought this whole thing through. Maybe being an heiress wasn't completely bad.

"And I," he said patiently, a smile lingering just beneath the surface and manifesting its presence in a sexy twitch of his lips, "explained to you that D'Martine Exports has a board of directors and an extremely competent CEO. You won't be expected to run any aspect of it. However, you will be expected to be aware of the operation of *your* company."

Her company? Now things were really getting bizarre. "Wait a minute!" She was on her feet before realizing she'd even moved. "I'm—"

A sudden banging at the front door cut off the rest of her intended tirade. "Eddi!"

"Ms. Mattie?" she muttered, a frown of confusion adding to the headache that had suddenly begun right between her eyes. Before she could get to the door, Doug was there checking it out, doing the bodyguard thing. His interference only made her headache that much worse.

Mattie Caruthers stood at Eddi's threshold, her twin sister, Minnie, as well as Ella Brown, clustered behind her. "Eddi, you have to help us. It's Irene, she fell and I think she's hurt."

Fear surged inside Eddi as she followed the ladies across her yard and around the row of hedges to her neighbor's driveway. Doug stayed right on her heels. Ms. Irene was no spring chicken anymore. If she'd fallen it could be serious. Vaguely, Eddi wondered what the ladies were doing at her neighbor's since he was out of town for the week.

"My dear, are you still with us?" Ella knelt next to Irene and took one hand in hers.

Irene groaned loudly.

Eddi's heart banged anxiously against her sternum. She rushed to the elderly lady's side. Mattie and Minnie were already gathered around her feet.

"Ms. Irene, tell me where it hurts," Eddi urged placatingly. They needed a phone. To call 911. An ambulance. That's what they needed.

"Oooooh," she wailed. "I can't breathe." Her right hand flew to her chest. "I think I need mouth-to-mouth resuscitation."

Baffled, Eddi leaned forward a bit. "You want me to—"

"Not you," Irene said petulantly. Her gaze shot to Doug, who was crouched next to Eddi. "Him!" she said with surprising fortitude.

Why, the woman wasn't hurt at all! Eddi glared at her. "Would you like some help getting up?" She should just go right back home and leave her lying there. Surely the former actress hadn't put on this whole shenanigan just for the attention.

Irene adopted a look of genuine displeasure. "Can't you see that I'm at death's door? I could go at any moment."

No wonder she'd won so many awards, Eddi thought wryly. But at the moment, she was not amused or impressed.

"I've had emergency medical training," Doug offered. "How about I make sure there are no broken bones and then we help you to your feet."

Ms. Irene smiled like the cat who'd swallowed the canary. "That sounds like exactly what we should do," she cooed.

Eddi wanted to shake her. She glared from one adoring face to the other. All four women were utterly and completely enamored of Mr. Douglas Cooper.

With Irene's skirt already hiked to the tops of her thighs, it was no problem for Doug to thoroughly check her limbs. Eddi was pretty sure she would have to stifle a gag reflex if the four uttered a gasp just one more time. One would think that each time Doug touched Irene he was laying hands on all four of them. By the time he was finished with his infuriatingly painstaking examination, Eddi wanted to barf.

"You feel just fine to me, ma'am," Doug said with that gracious charm that made Eddi's heart skip a beat even as annoyed as she was at the moment.

He assisted the smiling lady to her feet and made a show of helping her to dust away the leaves clinging to her clothing. "Dropping by your personal physician's office after taking a tumble like that would be advisable," he suggested when all was as it should be.

"Oh, I agree," Ella put in quickly. "That was quite a fall you took, Irene." She patted Doug on the back. "Why, what would we have done if this fine gentleman hadn't come along to help?"

Minnie and Mattie were next. Making over him as if he were the greatest thing to come along since sliced bread. As they bantered through the necessary introductions, it suddenly struck Eddi again that they were all standing in Mr. Curtis's driveway and that Irene's car was parked there.

"Ladies," Eddi said, breaking into the Dougfest, "what are you doing at Mr. Curtis's? Isn't he out of town?"

The hesitation that lasted less than a split second told the tale. They were spying on Eddi.

"Well, I...ah...we...he asked us to water his plants!" Mattie said, looking inordinately pleased that she'd come up with a plausible explanation.

Eddi braced her elbow on one arm and tapped her chin. "That's odd. He asked me to water his plants, too."

"Well," Mattie said nervously. The foursome exchanged doubtful glances and Minnie suddenly took up where Mattie had left off, "He knows how busy you get. We're just the backup plan in case you forget.'' Nervous laughter jittered back and forth between the four storytellers.

"You know how much the old goat loves those plants,'' Irene added for good measure. She turned her serene gaze back upon Doug then. "You must let me repay your kindness, sir,'' she urged in her best Scarlet O'Hara voice.

"That's not necessary, ma'am.'' Doug looked a little unnerved himself now. Eddi couldn't resist a smile.

"Oh, I won't take no for an answer.'' Irene's gaze flitted from Doug to Eddi and back where she batted her lashes dramatically. "You and Eddi come along over to my house tomorrow evening around six and we'll have dinner.''

Doug looked to Eddi for an answer but she wouldn't give him the satisfaction. She shrugged and left it at that.

"It'll be our pleasure,'' he responded, arrowing a little warning at her from the corner of his eye.

That's what he got for making such a production of examining the woman. Eddi's triumph died a sudden death when she recognized the feeling she'd just experienced—jealousy.

"Well,'' Ella piped up. "We should get you over to Doc Mathers.'' She ushered Irene toward the Cadillac. "He'll probably need to take X rays.''

The ladies called their goodbyes as they loaded into the old yellow vehicle that was in as close to mint condition as a car could be as it approached the half-century mark. Ms. Irene babied that car as if it were a child. Since she hadn't had any children of her own,

Eddi supposed that was the why of it. She kept her gaze carefully glued to the ladies until they'd disappeared from sight. She needed to do anything but think about the man standing next to her, and the last thing she needed was to be alone with him.

"Do they generally check up on you like this?"

Eddi nodded jerkily. "All the time." She had to regain her perspective here. She couldn't walk around behaving as foolishly as the matchmakers had. The fact that they had been spying on her lent credence to her fear that Doug's remark to Ms. Ada about dinner last evening had gone straight to the grapevine. If they ever found out he was staying at her place now— on the sofa, of course—she'd never convince them that he was just a bodyguard. Her anxiety moved to a new level. And then she'd have to tell them everything... How else could she explain having a bodyguard? Or a man sleeping at her house? She didn't know why she worried so. No one would ever believe that good girl Eddi Harper was being bad. She self-consciously straightened the suspenders of her overalls. Men didn't look at Eddi that way; everyone knew that.

This was getting too complicated. What did she need with a bodyguard? This D'Martine business wasn't even real to her. She was certain the whole thing had gotten blown out of proportion. What happened all those years ago had nothing to do with her. Well, okay...the man had been her biological father, but she hadn't even known him. She wasn't a D'Martine, not really. She should simply go meet her grandmother D'Martine, tell her how she felt and be done with it.

"I really have to get to work," she said, hoping to be rid of him for a while so she could think properly. Something about him interfered with her ability to process thought. "I'm behind from yesterday as it is. I'll check in with you at lunchtime, if you'd like."

"Sorry, Eddi, but it doesn't work that way." He splayed his hand in a gesture for her to precede him. "When I'm assigned to protect someone, it's 24/7. Don't you remember? We discussed that last evening along with your request for proper instruction."

Yesterday was one big, long blur of emotion. She scarcely remembered her own name, much less all that he'd told her. Okay, well, he had insisted on staying close by during his time here. Which, she supposed, made sense. If she was going to be vulnerable, nighttime would be the most likely time, she guessed.

She huffed a breath of impatience. She didn't like feeling vulnerable and she sure didn't like feeling all hot and bothered by some guy she barely knew. As for instruction, that might not even be necessary. Mrs. D'Martine might not even want her once she saw her.

"Heiress lessons will have to wait," she told him flatly. "I have real work to do."

EDDI HAD INSISTED THAT they take her truck. Her tools, after all, were in there. She couldn't work without her tools. Doug was reasonably sure after the first stop that she should learn a new line of work. She worked entirely too hard for too little. The fees she charged seemed woefully inadequate. But that was none of his concern so he kept quiet about it.

"Good morning, Mrs. Fairbanks," Eddi said cheerfully as they entered the home of her second customer of the day.

"I thought you'd forgotten about me," the elderly woman complained. "Called your daddy this morning and he said you'd be along." She spotted Doug then. "You training a new helper?"

Eddi smiled widely. Too widely. "Yes, ma'am, I sure am. This is Doug Cooper." She gestured to him and he nodded a hello. "He's learning the trade to supplement his income."

One gray eyebrow rose above the other as Mrs. Fairbanks divided a look between them. "You just make sure he does it right. I can't tolerate a faulty flusher."

"Not to worry," Eddi assured her. She patted him on the back then. "I'll watch every move he makes."

That statement instantly evolved into something else altogether. Him coming toward her...her lying naked on the bed waiting for him. Doug shook himself. He was relatively certain that scenario was not what she'd had in mind. Just as the next scenario to transpire had not been what he'd had in mind when he'd told her he would be her full-time shadow during this assignment.

"Hold it like that," she instructed.

The tiny closet in which the toilet was located simply had not been constructed for two. That Eddi had squeezed in beside him overseeing his first-ever flush-valve transplant was not conducive to productivity.

"This can't be the proper procedure," he protested, sweat rolling down his forehead. If she leaned forward and pressed her breasts against his arm just once more...

She did exactly that.

The tension in his muscles ratcheted up another notch.

"Just slide it into place." She leaned in closer still, putting her face nearer to his as he stared into the tank. "Just like that."

More words that made him think things he shouldn't. Forcing his attention to the task at hand, he pressed downward, locking the gadget into position.

"There you go." She beamed a smile up at him. "That was easy enough, wasn't it?"

He managed a curt nod. The temperature in the little closet shot up another ten degrees and he wondered if she had any idea how her proximity affected him. Mere centimeters separated their bodies and only in certain areas. Others were even closer. Not more than an inch or two stood between their faces. All she'd have to do is tilt up that determined little chin and he could kiss her.

He blinked, startled by his plunge toward doom.

"Are we finished?" The question was strained, but, considering he could hardly breathe much less speak, he thought he'd done fairly well.

"Just put the lid on the tank and that'll do it."

She left him to the chore and the temperature in the room dropped considerably, but the tension tightening his every muscle refused to abate. He would need a long, cold shower after this. He glanced at his watch and it wasn't even noon yet. How could a woman dressed in overalls and wielding a toolbox stimulate this much lust?

It simply didn't make sense.

Doug finished up and washed his hands in the basin before going in search of his charge. Well, at least now he knew how to replace a faulty fill valve. If he'd known one existed before today, it had escaped his memory. Or, more likely, he had banished the entire concept.

When Mrs. Fairbanks had settled her bill, Eddi loaded her toolbox into her truck and they headed toward the next stop of the morning.

"This is the sort of thing you do all day?" He really tried to keep the disbelief out of his tone, but he wasn't completely successful.

The grin on her face served as indication enough that he'd failed miserably. "Pretty much. It really gets interesting when you have to make a repair to the pipes in the crawl space under the house."

During his extensive personal-protection training he had been required to crawl through much worse than simply a dark place beneath someone's house, but the idea that this waiflike, fragile-looking young woman who could make him hard with just a look had done something vaguely similar, blew him away.

"I can imagine," was all he could think to say.

She turned right at the next street and parked in front of a small two-story frame house. When she'd shut off the engine, she turned to him and asked, "I know I don't represent the average sort of person who needs a bodyguard, but is this how you learned all about the way rich people behave? Being a body-guard, I mean."

Here was another sticky part. He didn't avoid her watchful gaze or she would know he wasn't being completely honest. Instead, he looked directly at her.

"In my work as an investigator and sometimes as a bodyguard, I often associate with the socially elite."

She nodded as she assimilated his answer. "So, I can take your advice to the bank. You know what you're doing? I won't end up looking stupid or anything?"

He had to smile at her utter innocence. She'd been thinking about what she needed to do. That was a step in the right direction.

"Trust me," he allowed. "I know all about the behavior patterns of the rich and famous."

That succulent, peach-ripe mouth of hers tilted into a smile of her own. Doug tamped down the nearly overpowering need to lean across the seat and taste her.

"Tonight," she promised, "we'll get down to business."

She shoved open her door and bounded out of the truck. Doug sat absolutely still for the space of three beats. He was certain her statement held no hidden meaning. He was positive she hadn't looked at his mouth with as much longing as he'd looked at hers.

But part of him wasn't convinced at all.

Chapter Five

By the time Eddi called it a day she was pretty sure Mr. Douglas Cooper had never before put in a full day of manual labor in his entire life. Not that he wasn't physically capable, mind you. He was that. A little shiver danced up her spine each time she considered just how physically capable he was. And not that he proved lazy either. He went out of his way to assist her and behaved as if he was taken aback by what she expected of herself. She was nearly positive he considered her line of work a man's job.

Well, it might traditionally be a man's occupation, but she was as good as any male plumber she'd ever had the occasion to run across.

No, her conclusion that Doug wasn't the manual-labor type had more to do with his sensibilities. He struck her as the sort of guy who did whatever necessary to accomplish his ultimate goal or mission. But he did so with entirely too much poise and grace not to stand out as different. Other than his clothing being a little more wrinkled and his hair ever so slightly mussed, he looked just as he had that morning.

She, on the other hand, looked a fright. Her overalls

were stained and stiff in spots where she'd gotten liquid Teflon glue all over her from one job. Then there was the greasy flux from the copper-pipe repair at Mr. Cagle's. Not to mention the sad state of the braid hanging a little lopsided down her back. She'd gotten it caught on a shut-off valve in a particularly tight spot inside a bathroom vanity. Doug had saved the day by untangling her hair since she'd had glue all over her hands. The way he'd had to reach in and blindly grope to get her hair loose still made her stomach flip-flop. God knew there'd hardly been room for her in there, his assistance had forced certain parts of his body to press against certain parts of hers. Whew! She'd scarcely survived the tension. It was definitely the most excitement she'd experienced since Tommy Hayden copped a feel senior prom night. And, she had to admit, she enjoyed Doug's inadvertent intimacy way more than she had Tommy's.

Eddi realized right then and there that the Club was right. She was pathetic…hopeless…doomed. At this rate she'd never land a boyfriend, much less a husband. Maybe those meddling old ladies were right about the family curse.

Twenty-five was only a few days away….

"Are we getting out?"

Doug couldn't say for sure whether Eddi was simply tired or if something else was wrong, but she looked up at him as if her whole world had just crashed in around her.

Damn, this new reality was finally sinking in, he presumed. He surveyed her disheveled appearance and admitted that she was still quite attractive in spite of it. But she was obviously overwhelmed by the news that her heritage was not what she'd thought it to be, and the most confusing and complicated was yet to come. She would never again know true privacy. Her every move, every word would be a matter of public scrutiny.

What she was about to face was the very thing he'd walked away from. He blinked and looked away, his stomach suddenly full of knots.

"Sorry...I was just thinking." She opened her door and got out, but her movements lacked her usual carefree flair.

Doug regretted that more than anything else. Though he'd only known her about twenty-four hours, he liked the old Eddi. The one who laughed with her customers and treated them as if they were family. He thought of the mother, Millicent, and the father, Harvey, who'd reared their daughter with such pride. The hurt he'd noted in their eyes would not be banished from his conscience for a long time to come. Then he considered Solange D'Martine. He wondered if she had any idea how much discomfort and uncertainty her desire to know Eddi was going to generate. The question as to whether or not she cared crossed his mind next.

As he followed Eddi inside her small cozy home his cell phone vibrated. He slipped it from his pocket and snapped it open just inside the front door.

"Cooper."

"Mrs. D'Martine would like an update."

Mr. Thurston. Impatient, demanding. It was somewhat less than reassuring to know that the man's personality was composed of so few facets. Doug had yet to see him display any other emotions.

"Things are going well," Doug reported, careful not to show his own impatience. He'd hardly been on the scene twenty-four hours. Mr. Thurston himself had only left that morning. What did he expect to have happened in the limited time that had passed since his departure?

"Mrs. D'Martine would like a definite date."

A scowl puckered Doug's forehead. "That decision has not been reached as yet."

"Look," Thurston huffed, "there is no reason to put off the inevitable. Mrs. D'Martine wants to see her granddaughter no later than Sunday. She would like to present the young lady in a public announcement on Thursday evening at the biannual gala."

"That's less than a week away," Doug argued. That wasn't enough time. There was too much she needed to know, to understand. "That's too soon."

Eddi paused on the other side of her living room and stared at him with worry etched across her face.

"Work it out. The board has decided to convene a special meeting on Wednesday," Thurston barked. "Make sure she's ready," he added before disconnecting.

Doug glared at the phone and considered throwing it across the room before he reined in his temper, closed the cell phone and put it away. He sighed and shook his head. Thurston had done just exactly what Doug was afraid he'd do. Now that the Harpers had been made aware of the D'Martines' discovery, the ball was rolling, the clock was counting down. The patience Thurston had proclaimed had vanished into thin air. They wanted what they wanted and they wanted it now.

"What was that about?" Eddi asked hesitantly. The expression on her face told him that she wasn't sure she cared to know.

Doug met that worried gaze and told her the truth, "The schedule just got pushed up. Your grandmother would like to see you on Sunday. There's some sort of special meeting scheduled with the board of directors on Wednesday and a gala on Thursday where she would like to publicly announce you as her granddaughter." He stiffened his spine and forced a more authoritative tone. "Can you be ready by then?"

She backed up a step, looking anywhere but at him now. "I need a shower. Let...let me think about this...." She did an about-face and disappeared down the hall.

Doug massaged his forehead with his fingers. A headache had suddenly begun there. There could be no more patiently waiting for her to make up her mind, he had to start preparing her immediately. No one could force her to do this, but if she decided to take the plunge he had to make sure she was ready. And if she refused, well, he had a feeling Thurston already had a backup plan in place. Now that the attorney's true colors had been exposed, Doug could see him leaking the news to the press and forcing Eddi to take a stand one way or the other.

Up until now Doug had primarily focused on preparing her for the media frenzy, but there was still the tainted kidnapping that hung over the D'Martine name. The idea that the original kidnapper was still out there and might try his hand again was a bit far-fetched in his opinion, but it wasn't completely impossible. Nor was the concept that someone new might attempt to do the same thing. The whole tragedy would be rehashed in the media, adding additional fuel to the possibility of a second attempt at milking the D'Martine fortune.

This had to be handled very carefully. Starting right now and starting with Eddi.

EDDI STRIPPED OFF her clothes and stepped beneath the warm spray of the shower. Once she'd shampooed, conditioned and rinsed her hair, she slumped against the cool aqua tile and allowed the emotions she'd been avoiding to consume her. How could she do this? How could she permit it to happen? The whole world would know the truth about who her father really was…and how would that make her dad feel? She had to consider his feelings. And what about her mother? How would she feel about the world knowing she'd gotten pregnant by one man and married another?

Squeezing her eyes shut to avoid the tears, Eddi told herself that she couldn't avoid the truth. Couldn't run away from reality. Mrs. D'Martine—her grandmother—wasn't going to let sleeping dogs lie. To an extent, Eddi could even understand how the woman felt. She'd lost her son, now she'd discovered that a part of her son still existed. Of course she wanted to be involved in Eddi's life. But at what cost?

Forcing herself to go through the motions of cleansing her body, she considered the other side of the coin, too. The money. If she accepted her destiny as the D'Martine heir, and assuming they all survived the media fallout, her parents would never again have to worry about money. The hardware store could be a relaxing hobby rather than an eked-out living. Her mother could afford the finest physical therapists and Eddi could always go to college.

She groaned. She'd never really wanted to go to college. Okay, well, maybe just a little. There had been no time and she hadn't exactly needed a degree to do her job. But Eddi knew that her parents desperately wanted her to have that opportunity. Eddi, on the other hand, could truthfully say she had no idea what she wanted to do with the rest of her life if it didn't include the hardware store and plumbing.

Who'd had time to really think about it? The last twenty-four hours had been a whirlwind of life-altering events. Besides, why would she have wasted the effort? Eddi had trained herself long ago not to wish for what she couldn't have…not to think about what was beyond her reach.

But now things had changed. That would take some getting used to. There were options.

Options that would bring pain to her family, she reminded herself as she shut off the faucet. She thought about that as she toweled herself dry. But, to a degree, the hurt had come anyway and she was pretty sure her grandmother D'Martine had no intention of backing off.

Eddi wrapped the towel around her and sat down on the closed toilet lid. She thought a while about Edouard D'Martine. Of how he'd loved her mother enough to go against his family and of how his life had been stolen from him at such a young age. Barely older than Eddi was right now. For the first time since learning the truth, her heart ached for the man who had been her biological father. His blood flowed through her veins and his heritage was hers if she wanted it…but she would never know him. She blinked away the sting of tears. It truly was a tragedy.

It would be selfish of her to exclude Solange D'Martine from her life, no matter what had happened in the past. Just as it would be selfish of her to turn her back on an inheritance from which her family would benefit greatly in the long run.

Eddi could be whoever she needed to be. If an heiress was the required role for keeping her *whole* family happy, then she could play the part. How bad could it be? With the extra money he would have, her father could hire a new plumber to serve the residents of Meadowbrook. Eddi could go to college…maybe. She'd find something to do.

It was the right thing.

She'd known that from the beginning or at least after the initial shock, but now she was considering both sides of the coin. Her grandmother D'Martine deserved a chance.

Eddi would give her that. Doing the right thing was what Eddi did best. As the disbelief—the shock—faded, more questions came. Like how did her grandmother finally learn about her? Eddi wanted more answers…soon.

After she'd slipped on a comfortable sweatshirt and running shorts, she tidied the bathroom, slinging her damp towel over the shower-curtain bar, and went in search of Doug.

She needed those lessons now. If she was going to do this, she definitely wanted to do it to the best of her ability. Making a fool of herself was not a notion she relished. No one made it through life, especially high-school years, without having a few moments of utter humiliation, but Eddi preferred to avoid it if possible.

Near the kitchen doorway she slowed. Doug had evidently searched her fridge and pantry for the makings of dinner. She found him chopping veggies for a salad. Inside the microwave her favorite frozen Italian entrée steamed as it slowly circled on the glass turntable.

Eddi opened her mouth to say something witty like, "Oh, the bodyguard cooks as well," but she deliberately closed it and took some time instead to observe her protector in silence and, unbelievably, without his knowledge.

The one thing she'd noted with a good measure of certainty in their brief time together was that Doug Cooper was intensely aware of his surroundings. A successful stealth approach would have required nothing short of a miracle, or so she would have thought. That she'd managed the feat only drove home the theory she'd harbored since meeting with the attorney this morning. Doug felt protective of her on more than a physical level. He didn't like the attorney's patronizing, pushy attitude. She hadn't missed the sympathy in his eyes on more than one occasion. For whatever reason, Doug fully empathized with her.

Interesting, she mused. That was, she felt certain, the source of his preoccupation. The very reason she stood here now watching him without his having noticed. Not that doing so was any sort of hardship. To the contrary; just looking at him was an exhilarating experience. He was more than simply handsome, which was the first thing she'd noticed. The great body added to the pleasing view. But it was much more than that. The way he moved, the way he spoke, even the way he looked at her made little flashes of heat flare deep inside her. She'd never looked at a man and felt precisely like this.

It had to be that whole turning-twenty-five-doomed-to-be-alone thing the matchmakers had started. They'd planted the seed and now she couldn't stop the gloom that had sprouted in her subconscious. Probably any guy with whom she'd been forced to spend time would have garnered the same reaction. Not that good-looking guys usually wanted to spend time with her.

Just then Doug looked up, his gaze collided with hers and heat seared straight through her.

Okay, so maybe just any guy wouldn't have ignited that kind of fire…but it was the principle of the thing. She was simply reacting to the subliminal message stuck in her brain. Her subconscious was fighting against the clock. Twenty-five and single was bad enough. But twenty-five and a virgin, well, that was beyond pathetic in the eyes of most. She just hadn't taken the time to think about it. She'd been too busy being a good daughter.

"I thought I'd make dinner," he said as he tossed the array of salad fixings into a big bowl. "Hope you don't mind."

She shook her head since speech was pretty much impossible. Her gaze kept wandering to those bare muscular forearms where he'd rolled up his sleeves. Then she made a visual path over his chest, past the cold steel weapon, until her gaze settled on the vee of tanned skin where his shirt lay open just enough to make her throat tighten and her breathing labored.

The telephone rang, saving her from certain humiliation since she just couldn't seem to stop staring at him. She crossed the room, her gaze now fixed firmly on the wall unit hanging next to the back door, and grabbed the receiver. "Hello."

"Eddi, dear, how are you this evening?"

Ms. Irene.

"Fine." She tried not to look at Doug now, to focus on the call. She really did, but it didn't work. "Is everything okay?" Her voice sounded entirely too high-pitched. Dear Lord, what had those old ladies done to her? She couldn't even think straight.

"Everything's just fine," Irene replied in that fake, too-accommodating voice she used when the mayor's wife called or one of the other town socialites she secretly despised but got along with nonetheless since social status meant power even in a small town like Meadowbrook, dropped by. "I only wanted to call and remind you of the dinner party you and that nice Mr. Cooper are invited to tomorrow evening."

Party? Since when had "dinner" turned into "party?" Irritation burned away the lust that had been playing havoc with Eddi's composure. "Dinner party? I thought you invited us to plain old dinner?"

"Well, now, don't get all worked up," Irene scolded good-naturedly. "I can't very well leave the others out. Six definitely makes it a party."

That was a little different. Eddi could tolerate the Club for a couple of hours. A sinking feeling suddenly tugged at her tummy. Oh, gosh. This wasn't about dinner or repaying Doug for his touchy-feely exam. This was another of their matchmaking schemes!

"Ms. Irene, don't you even think about—"

"Think about what?" She stalled Eddi's warning. "Is something wrong, dear? You sound positively distracted."

Ha! She wasn't going to get off that easily. "I just—"

Doug held up a glass and pointed to the iced-tea pitcher. Eddi nodded. "Thanks," she said to him, putting her hand over the receiver.

"Who are you talking to, Eddi?" Irene made a small knowing sound in her throat. "Do you have company? I didn't mean to intrude. I should let you go," she added in a rush.

Darn it! "No, no, Ms. Irene. I…I don't have company."

Doug tossed her a questioning look but quickly returned his attention to pouring her a tall glass of iced tea.

"To whom did you say thanks?" Irene pressed. "I distinctly heard you say thanks."

Eddi chewed her lower lip and racked her brain for a plausible explanation. "I was…about to eat. I had to say grace and since I was in a hurry…because I'm starving and trying to talk to you…I…ah…just skipped to the chase and said thanks."

Silence echoed across the line for a second or two.

"Well, in that case I won't keep you," Irene said suspiciously. "Enjoy your dinner and don't forget about tomorrow evening, six sharp."

Eddi hung up the receiver and scrubbed both hands over her face. She checked the claw clip holding her still-wet hair and commanded her heart rate to slow before allowing her gaze to meet the one now staring a hole through her.

"I'm not sure I want to know what that was about."

Eddi clasped her hands together in front of her and cautiously approached the counter where he worked. "There's something you should know about Ms. Irene and her friends."

Doug inclined his head a bit to the right and waited for her to clarify the statement.

"They have this club." She swallowed back the tension rising in her throat. "It's called—" she shrugged "—the Club."

"How original," he offered, sparing her only a brief assessment with those heart-stopping blue eyes as he arranged salad onto two plates.

"Anyway, they get together every Wednesday and have a poker game."

One dark eyebrow arched above the other. "Poker?"

She nodded. "They discuss all the town gossip and drink a little homemade Remedy, which is about one hundred proof." She turned her hands palms up. "Smoke a few cigars."

Doug stopped transferring greens from the bowl to a plate and looked directly at her. "We *are* talking about the ladies from the incident this morning?"

She nodded again.

He made a circling motion with his left hand in a tell-me-the-rest gesture. "This Remedy, is it legal?"

She moved her head side to side. "Not in this county."

"I see." He finished with the salads and carried the plates to the small table near the window.

"So yesterday the topic of discussion was me," she admitted, automatically following his lead. Might as well make herself useful. She collected the dressing from the fridge and the necessary silverware.

Once the two glasses of iced tea were on the table, he held a chair for her and asked, "They don't know about—"

"Oh, no." She took the seat he offered and smiled in thanks. "It wasn't about that."

He sat down directly across from her and waited for her to continue.

She shrugged. "It was nothing really. There's just this curse in my family—"

"Curse?" He looked more than skeptical.

She bobbed her head up and down. "If I don't marry before I'm twenty-five I'm doomed to spend the rest of my life alone." She plastered a smile in place. "Silly, isn't it?"

His answer was so slow in coming she wasn't sure he intended to comment. "Yes," he finally said. "Is there some basis for this thinking?"

"I've had several female relatives who suffered from the plight." God, could this sound any more lame? "So, the Club is convinced that I'm headed for trouble."

He studied her for a while. So long that Eddi felt the need to squirm. "I don't think you have anything to worry about, Eddi. You're a beautiful young woman. Finding a man willing to spend the rest of his life with you won't be a challenge." He smiled, that silky, all-charm expression that made her nerves jangle and her insides too hot. "You can take that to the bank as well."

She sprang to her feet, almost overturning her chair. "You know, I'm not really hungry. I think I'll make an early night of it." She hated not to eat the dinner he'd gone to the trouble to prepare, but she just couldn't do this. She blinked repeatedly and then somehow managed to meet his gaze. "Good night."

"Eddi."

She stalled at the door. She did not want to turn around. She didn't want to look at him. She didn't want to hear his voice. Somehow she had to get out of her head this crazy notion those matchmaking old biddies had planted. It was making her act completely out of character.

Dredging up courage from some source deep inside her that she hadn't known existed until then, she turned around. He stood at the table, just looking at her with a patience and understanding that defied reason.

"When you're ready we need to talk about your plans. You can't keep putting this off."

She swallowed tightly. He was right. She had to do this. She couldn't run from it. "Tell them I'll be there on Sunday." She started to turn away, but looked back at him once more. "I guess we should start those heiress lessons tomorrow."

Then she went to bed. Curled up with those things that were familiar to her like her favorite blanket and the ragged teddy bear pillow she'd had for as long as she could remember, and ordered herself to sleep.

She had responsibilities. Obligations.

She didn't have time for foolish matchmaking games.

Or for her first case of pure, undeniable lust.

That's all this could be, she told herself as she drifted off. She was no princess and Doug was no knight in shining armor.

Chapter Six

"Doesn't your mother drive a gray sedan?" Doug wanted to know early the next morning as he peeked between the wood shutters to see who'd pulled up in the driveway.

Eddi forgot that she was having the worst bad-hair day in history, gave up the search for her favorite cap and strode over to the window. She frowned as she peered out through the slats. It was her mom. What the heck was she doing out this early? She hardly ever left the house. Worry that something had happened suddenly tied a neat little knot in Eddi's stomach.

"What's happened now?" she muttered as she unlocked the door. Enough already, she wanted to rant.

Eddi hurried down the two steps that separated the small stoop from the yard and over to the driver's side of her mother's car. "You're certainly an early bird," she said cheerily, hoping to offset some of the dread already rising to panic proportions.

Milly took her daughter's offered hand and pulled herself from the driver's seat. Bracing her weight on her cane, she hobbled far enough out of the way for Eddi to close the car door. "I want to talk," her mother said. "I've been up most of the night mulling things over."

"Come on inside, Mom," Eddi urged. The last thing she wanted was for any of this to worry her mother. But hoping that it wouldn't was unrealistic.

"Good morning, Mrs. Harper."

Eddi hadn't even noticed that he'd followed. But, of course, he had. He was a bodyguard after all. It was his job to follow her body wherever it went. The thrilling sensation that shot through her at that thought made her just a little giddy. She forced away the idea. She had to stop thinking like that. But, her emotions had always ruled her. She doubted that would change this side of the grave.

"Good morning, Mr. Cooper."

"Doug," he insisted.

As he followed Eddi and her mother back into the house she suddenly wondered about his parents and where he lived. They hadn't discussed *him* at all. But then, this wasn't about him, was it?

No matter how she tried, it always came back to those silly emotions she shouldn't be allowing.

Once she'd settled her mother on the sofa, Eddi selected the same seat she'd occupied the day before when she and Doug had talked. He graciously offered to make a fresh pot of coffee, which gave them some privacy.

"All right." Eddi folded her hands in her lap. "Let's talk." Her mother was staring at her now…really staring at her as if she'd never seen her before. Eddi wondered if she was seeing for the first time in a long while the D'Martine traits. Doug had told her she was the image of her grandmother.

"Oh, Eddi, you do look so like your…like Edouard." Her mother glanced away but her smile didn't fade. "Your father and I have worked hard all these years to put that behind us." Her eyes met Eddi's once more. "But it's time you knew that part of who you are." She sighed wistfully. "I suppose I was wrong for keeping this from you so long—"

Whoa. Been there, done that. "Mom, Dad and I already had this discussion. I'm glad you waited. You did the right thing."

Milly leaned back fully in her chair and rested her cane across her lap. "Your father and I don't want you to miss out on all the things we did. Your grandmother D'Martine can give you so much more. The past is over. It's time to get on with our lives. Twenty-five years is a long time to keep secrets. Too long."

Eddi was still hung up on the part about all her parents had missed. She knew about her mom…. "Mom, you left college and never went back because you were pregnant with me. Did Dad—"

She nodded. "Your father had a full scholarship to the college over in Aberdeen. But you can't do college with a brand-new family." Realization of what she'd revealed belatedly dawned. "Oh, but we've never regretted our decision for a moment." She leaned forward, wincing with the effort. "Please don't think that. It was hard, yes. But you and the life we've had have been worth every moment."

That was the one thing Eddi didn't doubt. Still, she couldn't help feeling bad that her mom and dad had given up so much to take care of her. That news only strengthened her resolve to go forward with her decision.

"I'm flying to Martha's Vineyard to meet her—Grandmother D'Martine—on Sunday," Eddi announced. There, that was said. Her mother didn't say anything, she simply looked at her. "Doug will be going with me...to make sure I'm okay," Eddi added in hopes of prodding a response from her mom.

"As much as it hurts to see you go," her mother said after a while, "I do believe it's the right thing."

Doug arrived with the coffee just then. Eddi was glad for the reprieve. Her mother's eyes were a little bright and Eddi was sure her own were as well.

"I have a few calls to make," he said before disappearing back into the kitchen.

Watching him walk away, Eddi narrowly caught herself before she sighed out loud.

Her mom looked from her to Doug and back. "Sweetie, is there something I should know?" she prompted.

Eddi snapped to attention and shook her head a little too vigorously. "No. No. Nothing. That's what bodyguards do, you know. Make you feel at ease." She gestured to the cups of steaming coffee on the table. "And make coffee."

That seemed to placate her mother, thank God.

"Your father and I will expect to hear from you every day," she said firmly, but Eddi didn't miss the hint of a quake in her voice.

"I'll call every day."

"I'll prepare a photo album for you to take along," she went on.

"A photo album?" That one kind of flew right over Eddi's head.

"I'm sure your grandmother D'Martine will want to see pictures of you through the years."

"Oh." Eddi nodded then. "Good idea." She wouldn't have thought of that until she'd gotten there and the woman asked for that very thing.

"Don't worry about your father or the store. Lamar Parks is going to fill in for you while you're gone."

Something resembling outrage ruptured inside Eddi at the mention of Lamar's name. "Momma, couldn't it be anybody but him." She just didn't like the guy. His work was passable but he was just so obnoxious and always competing with Eddi.

"You don't worry about that. Your father will take care of the business. You have other things to attend to right now." Her mom smiled. "You can be anything you want to, little girl. Don't hold back."

Overwhelmed by her mother's unconditional support, Eddi deftly changed the subject. And she'd worried about any of this hurting her parents. She could go to Martha's Vineyard now with a clear conscience.

An epiphany abruptly took root. So, that's what this was all about. Her mother intended to make sure that no force on earth held her daughter back from taking this next step. Well, Milly and Harvey Harper had no legitimate worries. Nothing or no one would ever replace them in Eddi's heart.

FAUCET PARTS WERE scattered across the counter like the site of a downed aircraft. Doug didn't see any way Eddi would ever get the thing back together again. When he would have said as much, she whipped around and made her first demand.

"This is Friday. I only have forty-eight hours."

Her horrified gaze locked with his. "Are you sure I can do this? I mean, what if I say or do the wrong thing?"

Eddi had been too quiet since her mother's visit that morning. Doug felt reasonably sure that she'd needed to think, so he'd left her to her silence.

"You'll make mistakes," he granted. "Some things can't be taught, you simply have to learn them by trial and error."

She tossed aside the rubber seals she'd just dug from her toolbox. "What kind of questions will the media ask me?"

He could see her anxiety level double with every question as it occurred to her. Time to put the brakes on the fear factor. "There's no way to know for certain. I would imagine they'll ask about your childhood and growing up in Meadowbrook. But that won't be the first topic of discussion."

Worry knitted its way across her forehead. "It won't?"

He propped against the kitchen counter and adopted a completely relaxed stance in hopes that she would as well. "First they'll want to know how you came to be a D'Martine. They'll concentrate on that topic for a while. Mrs. D'Martine's publicist will likely release a statement in regards to that subject in advance."

Her eyes rounded slightly. "She has a publicist?"

"At least one, maybe two."

Chewing on her lower lip as she so often did, Eddi twirled a strand of hair on her finger. Her usually smooth braid was a little frazzled-looking today. She complained a full twenty minutes about not being able to find her cap. Doug supposed even plumbers had bad-hair days. But right now, all he could think about was how much he'd like to be nibbling on that full bottom lip.

"All I have to do is answer the questions truthfully and I'll be okay." She looked relieved by her conclusion.

"Unless the publicist or attorney tells you not to divulge certain information," he countered. That was a very likely scenario considering the facts.

Uncertainty once more claimed Eddi's pretty face. "I've never been very good at lying. Mom and Dad caught me every single time I tried."

Doug passed a hand over his jaw to cover his smile. He'd just bet she couldn't tell a lie if her life depended upon it. He'd have to warn Thurston about that.

"The key," he told her, "with the media is to stay calm and relaxed. They'll pick up on it if you're nervous. Think about something that makes you feel calm and focus on that while the circus goes on around you." That's what he'd always tried to do and it worked most of the time.

She retrieved the seals and proceeded to insert them into some part of the faucet that Doug couldn't name. "All I have to do is stay cool and I'll be fine. Okay," she said more to herself than to him. "I can do that."

In two minutes flat she had the faucet completely reassembled. Amazing. He'd have sworn it was a hopeless case. But there it was, drip free.

"Wait." She closed the lid on her toolbox and turned back to him. "Do I have to walk a certain way? Dress differently?"

The walk was just fine, he mused. And he had noticed. The dress? He surveyed her overalls. Now that was another story.

She rolled her eyes. "I know I can't go dressed like this, but I don't think I have anything else appropriate either." She popped herself on the forehead with the heel of her hand. "What am I saying? I know I don't have anything appropriate."

Before another look of doom could set in on her expression, Doug hefted the toolbox and assured her, "No problem. We'll go shopping tomorrow."

"I didn't know bodyguards took you shopping, too."

He smiled over his shoulder at her. "I'm a different kind of bodyguard."

Outside, Eddi walked with her shoulders squared and her chin held high. "Like this, right?"

"Not quite so stiffly," he pointed out. "Your usual walk is fine. Just remember not to look down and to keep smiling."

She smiled widely and started a perfect Miss America wave. "Am I good or what?"

Neighbors started to wave back. "See!" Eddi teased. "I have fans already."

Doug placed the toolbox in the back of the truck and opened the door for her. "Not fans, Eddi," he chided. "Admirers."

She scowled at him as she slid across the bench seat and settled behind the steering wheel. "Doesn't that mean the same thing?"

He hesitated before dropping into the passenger seat. "Admirers admire." His tone turned grim then.

He couldn't have stopped it had he tried. "Fans fixate, they accost. Take it from someone who knows."

All signs of amusement disappeared, but Doug turned his attention forward, away from those questioning eyes. He'd said too much. She'd read between the lines. Now she would want to know more.

And he couldn't give her more.

THE BAD-HAIR DAY had morphed into an all-out-appearance catastrophe. Eddi finally had her hair under some semblance of control. Whether it was the new shampoo she'd tried or the new conditioner, not a single strand had wanted to go in the same direction as the other. Now the challenge was wardrobe. She'd wasted her only real chance at looking elegant that first night she and Doug had gone to dinner. Now there was little to choose from.

Frustrated, she glanced at the bedside clock: 5:40. She had to hurry. No wonder she didn't bother dating, not that anyone had been asking. It was too much trouble. Too much stress. And this wasn't even a real date.

She silently repeated that last statement a dozen times over but it didn't change the fact that tonight felt like a date, just as the first time they'd gone to dinner had.

"Because you're hopeless," she said to her reflection as she held one last wardrobe offering against her chest. "And doomed to spend your life alone with nothing to wear."

Eddi sighed and resigned herself to wearing the hideous green skirt and matching vest she'd owned for half a lifetime. The only reason it still fit was because she'd had that sudden growth spurt in seventh grade and had spent the next three years a full head taller than even the boys in her class. The upside was that she could still wear the same clothes.

Left with little choice, she wiggled into the green skirt and its matching blouse. The pale-mint blouse was the only thing that had changed about the ensemble since its original purchase. The blouse she liked. It was silky and feminine-looking. The overall effect, she decided as she stepped back to view her reflection, she could live with. But the vest was out.

Not that Doug would notice what she wore. She was a case…a principal as he called her. He probably didn't even see her as a woman.

Eddi stilled, one shoe on, one off. This was the first time she'd thought of herself as a woman in more years than she could remember. She was Eddi, the plumber. Her daddy's little girl. Mom's best helper. Everybody's good friend. But she was no one's lady…girlfriend…or lover.

The matchmakers were right. She was cursed.

Any sensuality she'd ever possessed had vacated the premises a few hundred leaky-faucet repairs ago.

Eddi looked at herself again and shrugged. Oh well, she was a good plumber, a good daughter and a good friend. A good girl. That was something this day and time.

Doug waited in the living room, his attention on the photographs scattered along the mantel.

When she walked into the room he looked up and smiled. Every fiber of femininity in her soul stirred.

Damn, she mused. Maybe she was more woman than she'd realized.

"Very nice," he commented as his gaze slowly slid down the length of her. When his eyes met hers she didn't miss the glimmer of approval there.

Oh, hell yes. She was woman.

Eddi's eyes rounded and she bit down hard on her lower lip. What was wrong with her? She never swore. The occasional darn or dang was about the extent of her trash talk. She hadn't gone to church every Sunday her entire life for nothing.

"Shall we?" Doug moved in close and offered his arm.

Something in her chest bounced. Her heart, she was pretty sure. Her arm looped through his of its own accord and the resulting physical reaction was nothing short of breath stealing. As if that wasn't enough he leaned closer and inhaled deeply. "Mmm. You smell nice, too."

She pushed a smile into place and expelled a strangled thank-you as her eyes took in his every detail from head to toe. The hair was perfect, what else could she say? Thick, dark, wavy. The eyes...well, the eyes were simply hypnotic. The light blue shirt and navy trousers and jacket fit as if they were tailor made for him. And, talk about sexy—the way he smelled was absolutely sinful.

By the time he'd opened the door to his SUV and assisted her inside, she'd gone into total meltdown.

She forced herself to look straight ahead and to breathe deeply. The entire five minutes it took to get to Ms. Irene's house was spent this way and still it did no good. She couldn't get the idea of sex out of her head. She couldn't stop thinking about how his scent...his touch...those eyes.

And she wanted more.

Once he'd parked, before she could open her door he was already there, opening it for her, taking her hand. When her feet at last settled back on the ground, every square inch of her was on fire.

"What a waste," she murmured before she could catch herself.

He hesitated at Ms. Irene's front door. "Excuse me?"

Eddi shook her head and shrugged simultaneously. "I was just thinking about all those Sundays I've spent in church."

A frown marred those devilishly handsome features. "That's the waste that concerns you?"

She nodded, and at the same time the door opened she muttered, "Yeah, 'cause I'm going to hell anyway."

"Eddi! Doug! You're here," Irene gushed. "Come in, please."

Feeling utterly confused, Doug allowed himself to be dragged through the door by Mrs. Marlowe. Before he could question Eddi's strange comment, he was surrounded by Mrs. Marlowe, Mrs. Brown and the Caruthers sisters.

As Doug soon learned, Mrs. Marlowe had once been all the rage on the big screen. Must have been before his time. Ella Brown was a former schoolteacher and the Carutheres had been blessed with a sizable inheritance and were never forced to take on a career.

Eddi stayed in the background, laughing at all the right times, but behaving more nervously than Doug had ever seen her. He told himself that it was the pending trip to Martha's Vineyard and meeting her grandmother for the first time that had her out of sorts, but that didn't feel right. Every time their eyes met she looked away. Had he said or done something that offended her or made her uncomfortable? He considered his every move this evening and then he nailed it. The remark about how good she smelled. She'd behaved oddly since. An apology would be in order as soon as they had a moment alone.

If that ever happened.

"Escort me to the dining room," Irene ordered, taking Doug by the arm and ushering him in the right direction.

When he had seated the ladies, including Eddi, who reacted stiffly to his slightest touch, Doug sat down across from her. He smiled but she turned away. Damn, the woman was frustrating. And he was an idiot. He should be glad that she was keeping him at bay. He'd certainly lost most of his perspective where she was concerned. He'd let what started out as a harmless attraction get out of control.

If he was smart, he'd use her indifference tonight to regain some lost ground. But every time he looked at her, traced the outline of that delicate cheek with his eyes, stared at that lush mouth—

"So, Doug, where do you call home?" Irene asked, shattering the forbidden trance he'd drifted into.

"Chicago," he replied, railing at himself silently for allowing yet another incident of distraction. His first lead assignment and already he was screwing it up.

Irene frowned dramatically. "Chicago. Hmm. What do you do for a living?"

Eddi coughed indelicately. Her wide-eyed gaze collided with Doug's.

"I'm in research," he fudged, knowing without the little coughing jag that Eddi didn't want to reveal anything just yet.

Ella was the next to jump into the inquisition. "How interesting? What do you research?"

The teacher in her, no doubt. No one else would have asked that question since he had not offered to elaborate.

"I do investigative research on people. Their backgrounds, finances. Things like that."

Minnie and Mattie Caruthers exchanged guarded looks.

"You don't work for the IRS, do you?" Mattie speculated.

Doug smiled. What were those two up to? "No, ma'am. I don't work for the government at all. I work for a private agency."

Their look of relief was almost comical. Even Eddi hinted at a smile.

"Tell us, Douglas," Irene said suspiciously, "what are your intentions toward our Eddi."

Eddi's soupspoon clattered into her bowl.

All four members of the Club leaned forward awaiting his response.

He looked to Eddi for guidance. Now, he estimated, looked like a good time to simply tell the truth.

"She is rather naive, Douglas," Ella Brown pressed when he was slow to answer. "It's our duty to protect her interests. If your intentions are not honorable—"

"Ms. Ella!" Eddi butted in. "It's not what you think. It's—"

"She's a virgin, you know," Minnie Caruthers explained with a pitying glance at Eddi.

Eddi wanted to die.

This was her punishment. She'd permitted bad thoughts and this was the recompense. The look, something between shock and disbelief, on Doug's face completed her mortification.

With lightning speed he recovered, the mask of composure falling back into place. "Ms. Caruthers, I assure you—"

Eddi held up her hands stop-sign fashion. She couldn't let this go any further. "Ladies, you don't understand." She swallowed or attempted to, her muscles didn't want to cooperate. At least now she had everyone's attention. Doug looked eternally grateful that she'd stepped in. She wondered how grateful he'd be in about thirty seconds.

"Doug isn't here to court me," she explained. The ladies' mouths formed perfect O's of confusion. "No, no, I'm sorry to disappoint you. He's an old friend I met in…in Baltimore that time I visited." She had gone to Baltimore once. A long time ago. "He's on a business trip and just passing through. Since we're old friends and all, I figured it wouldn't be right to leave him in that old boardinghouse. You know how nosy Ms. Ada is." She forced a strained laugh, but no one else made a sound. Even Doug's smile looked pinned in place.

"Anyway," she went on, too late to turn back now.

"You ladies don't have to worry about what's going on between Doug and me 'cause there just isn't anything going on." She shrugged helplessly. "'Cause… 'cause he's gay."

Chapter Seven

Eddi stood in the middle of her bedroom and stared at the door. She had to go out there eventually. Had to face Doug. She'd hardly slept at all last night for worrying about what he would say to her once he started speaking to her again.

She closed her eyes and exhaled a disgusted breath. Why on earth had she told the ladies in the Club that he was gay? Why hadn't she simply told them the truth? Eddi walked over to the door and rested her forehead against it. Because it was too hard…too confusing. And telling anyone outside the family would make it too real.

So she'd said the first thing that came to mind to throw the matchmakers off the Cupid game.

She would never, ever forget the look of startled disbelief on Doug's face. He surely thought she was just the most horrible, selfish, thoughtless person on the planet. With another sigh Eddi grasped the doorknob. She couldn't stay in here forever. Today was the big shopping day. Tomorrow they would leave for Martha's Vineyard, assuming Doug wasn't so mad at her that he'd decided to resign from her case. Real anxiety twisted inside her at that thought. She couldn't do this without him. Silly as it sounded, she trusted him. It didn't matter that she scarcely knew him. She simply trusted him. He'd spent time around the financially blessed. He knew all the answers, or at least more than she did. With his guidance she might just get through this.

She stood tall and squared her shoulders. Her only choice was to apologize profusely and beg his forgiveness. The longer she put it off the tougher it would be.

She opened the door with a firm twist of the knob and marched straight to the living room where Doug waited at the dining table, a cup of fresh-brewed coffee in hand.

"I'm sorry I told Ms. Irene and her friends that you're gay," she said without stopping to think or giving herself time to back out. "I had to derail their matchmaking scheme." She set her hands on her jean-clad hips. "It was your own fault anyway for starting this mess with that whole dinner thing the first day you arrived."

His deadpan expression never changing, he set his coffee aside and smiled. "Good morning to you, too."

Good morning? Was that all he had to say? Ire kindled deep in her belly. After she'd tossed and turned all night? For goodness' sakes, he hadn't spoken another single word to her during the rest of dinner or the ride home last night. He hadn't even said good-night and all he could say now was *good morning*?

"I lost a whole night's sleep and all you have to

say is good morning?'' she demanded, giving voice to her growing irritation.

The smile broadened across those sinfully full lips. ''I'd say we're even.''

Her mouth dropped open in astonishment. He'd done that on purpose! He'd wanted her to toss and turn all night. He'd...

Okay, maybe she'd deserved that at the very least.

''No hard feelings?'' she entreated, feeling contrite all over again for her thoughtlessness.

Doug wasn't sure how to answer that one. To say she engendered no hard feelings in him would be an outright lie. *Hard* appeared to be his new watchword. The remark about his being gay...well, he certainly hadn't appreciated it but his confidence in his own masculinity wasn't so fragile that he couldn't take the occasional blow to his ego. Especially since he knew that she knew better.

As to the hard feelings, there were some things she didn't need to know. ''None,'' he lied for her benefit.

All he had to do was look at her and his sexual preference made itself well known. Case in point, if he didn't know how sincere and innocent Eddi was, he'd swear that she'd dressed this morning with torture in mind. But he knew better than that. The tight-fitting jeans probably had a lot more to do with frugality than fashion. The material was worn soft with age and use. The torso-hugging pale yellow blouse provided an arousing preview of what lay beneath the T-shirt and baggy overalls she usually donned. She wore her long hair down today and the D'Martine streak of white looked softer somehow, far less stark than when she kept that thick mane pulled back into a braid. Yet, her manner of dress could in no way be defined as seductive and, still, it was exactly that.

He moistened his lips and forced himself to take another sip of coffee just to distract his wayward thoughts. Today, he mused, in spite of his best efforts not to, plumber Eddi Harper looked sexy. Young and sexy, he reminded that wicked little voice in his head. Young and virginal.

Eddi wasn't the only one who hadn't gotten any sleep last night. He'd already developed a serious case of "unobjectivity" where his principal was concerned. Neither the braid nor the overalls or even the toolbox had stopped him from developing a healthy case of lust where this little plumber was concerned. He'd tried hard not to look at her as a woman...but it hadn't worked. Had failed miserably, in fact.

And now, well, suffice it to say that he had his work cut out for him today if he planned to do the job for which he'd been hired. Since this was the first major assignment of his new career, he'd damned well better do it right. Victoria Colby prided herself in the integrity of her agents. He wasn't about to let her down. Or Eddi.

"Are you ready to go shopping?" he asked as he pushed to his feet and ordered his brain to reroute any forbidden thoughts to some dark side of his mind where they belonged. "There's more coffee."

"None for me, thanks." She smiled, sending a new jolt of desire straight to his loins. "I'm ready to get this show on the road."

"Very well then." His movements uncharacteristically awkward, he carried his cup to the kitchen and turned off the coffeemaker.

All he had to do was get through this day and the coming night. Once they were in Martha's Vineyard, under the close regard of Thurston and Mrs. D'Martine, keeping his perspective would be considerably less difficult. Not to mention that he would need to be more on guard for any threat to Eddi, as well as himself. The paparazzi were never far away from a name like D'Martine. Keeping his face out of the limelight wasn't going to be a simple task.

But keeping Eddi safe was his first priority.

The moment her connection to the D'Martine name became headlines, so would her value as a tradable commodity in the media.

DOUG DROVE TO A LARGER, nearby city and quickly discovered a small cluster of exclusive shops. One or two of the names he didn't recognize, but he knew the look—high credit limits required. Since Mr. Thurston had directed that Eddi be prepared in every way, Doug felt no hesitation in shopping for the best.

"We should go to the mall," Eddi suggested, looking a little worried that he'd parked in front of one of the exclusive shops. "This place is—"

"Exactly what we're looking for," he countered. "I have Mrs. D'Martine's authorization to purchase whatever you require for your debut."

Eddi's forehead scrunched into a scowl. "Get real, Doug. It isn't like I'm some celebrity."

He shook his head in regret of just how little she understood in regards to what was about to happen. He'd tried to get the point across to her, but there was really no way to make her comprehend how much her life was about to change.

Eddi didn't like how this was going. She didn't shop at places like this, but she followed him inside just the same. This was his ball game and the only thing she could do was play. She had to trust his judgment.

An elegantly dressed woman seized their attention before the door even closed behind them. "Good morning." Those glossy lips stretched into a wide, welcoming smile. "How may I help you?" Her smile slipped just a bit when she got a better look at Eddi, but quickly pushed back into full bloom for Doug. A snob. Eddi knew it before she even walked in the door.

The next few minutes proved somewhat mind-boggling for Eddi. Doug gave instructions and the sophisticated saleslady jumped to obey. She seated Doug in a comfortable-looking overstuffed chair in a large mirrored room. Four doors, each leading to a huge dressing room, were strategically placed about the circular space. At first, Eddi merely stood in the center of the room while the saleslady measured and estimated the proper size.

"Oh, yes, just as I thought," the older woman murmured to herself. "A size four."

Eddi could have told her that if she'd only asked. Without further ado, the saleslady, who identified herself as Doris, flew into a frenzy of garment gathering. She then held offering after offering in front of Eddi. The wardrobe offerings weren't for Eddi's benefit; the full and undivided attention of the saleslady was focused on Doug. A simple, negligent nod of encouragement would send the woman scurrying for yet another selection.

When she had at last produced a dozen or so acceptable ensembles ranging from slacks-and-sweater combinations to skirts and matching blazers, she ushered Eddi into the spacious dressing room and started the next phase.

Her stomach twisting with tension and her nerves frayed beyond reason, Eddi, with the assistance of the saleswoman, slipped into one outfit after another, then traipsed around the showroom for Doug's entertainment.

By the fourth outfit Eddi was furious. His expression never changed. That frustratingly scrutinizing gaze followed her every move, thoroughly raked her body, but not once did she see even a glimmer of particular interest one way or the other. She felt like a horse at auction where the buyers endeavored to keep their intentions unknown until all the bids were placed.

He simply watched, assessed and gave one succinct nod or shake of his head by way of a final decision. He made no comments, which infuriated Eddi all the more. She knew it was ridiculous. That it made no sense whatsoever. But she wanted to know what he really thought.

Did she look okay? Didn't that last outfit make her look fat? She'd always heard that redheads weren't supposed to wear pink. What was up with the pastel-pink slacks outfit? She had liked it, that was true…but…she sighed. What did she know about what did or didn't look chic? That determination, she supposed, was best left to the discriminating taste of the saleslady and the man in charge.

Finally, Eddi wore the last outfit and stood waiting

for Doug's yea or nay. Abruptly he motioned for the saleslady, just the slightest twitch of his fingers and she rushed to his side as if he were the Messiah and was about to tell her of the Second Coming.

Eddi's gaze narrowed as she watched the woman lean in closer for Doug to whisper something in her ear. The hag. She was flirting with him. Eddi was certain her breasts must be brushing his arm the way she hovered over him. Well, she fumed as she folded her arms over her chest, some people would do anything for a commission.

"Yes, sir," the lady enthused and hurried away.

Eddi glowered at Doug, who still sat in that stupid chair looking at her. "What's she going for now?" Eddi's right foot started to tap. She gritted her teeth and forced the tapping to stop. "Surely all this is enough."

"The pièce de résistance," Doug informed her in that all-silk-and-charm voice that made her heart beat a little faster, despite her current annoyed state.

Before Eddi could ask what he meant, the woman rushed back into the room with what looked like a ball gown. "How is this, sir?"

She held the gown under Eddi's chin and waved her arm as if to say *voilà*. Doug nodded in that same vague yet somehow succinct motion.

"Let's try it on," the saleslady urged, propelling Eddi toward the dressing room.

Doug waited, not moving, scarcely drawing a breath. He wasn't sure he could tolerate one more moment of watching Eddi twirl around in those ultra-feminine ensembles. To merely say she looked beautiful in each and every one would have been a gross injustice. His entire body had tensed to the point of pain simply looking at her. With the overalls, toolbox and braid out of the way, she was incredibly beautiful. Her sweet innocence only added to the perfection. It seemed that even without the elite upbringing, posh prep schools and haughty attitude, Eddi had the makings of the right stuff—an infinite grace and beauty that came straight from the heart and soul.

She was extraordinary.

But he had to stop thinking about her that way.

Just then the dressing-room door opened and she stepped out. His breath stalled somewhere in the vicinity of his chest and he was sure his heart had stopped beating altogether.

The gown was simple and yet more elegant than anything he'd ever seen. Strapless and formfitting, it flowed down those long legs as if it had been designed with her in mind. The rich fabric and royal-blue color were exquisite. It was perfect...just as she was.

"That's the one," he said, surprised at his ability to actually speak.

"Wonderful," the saleslady cheered, most likely tabulating her grand commission already. "Will there be anything else?"

Eddi's expression turned to one of absolute misery. She was the only woman Doug had ever met who didn't care for power shopping.

"We'll need all the accessories," he directed. "*All* the accessories."

EDDI HADN'T KNOWN UNTIL today that it was possible to buy matching underwear for every outfit. But it was. She now owned enough silky, lacy undergarments to last a lifetime, not to mention shoes and matching purses for every single getup, even the gown. Heck, the saleslady had even insisted upon jeweled barrettes and clips for her hair. Then there had been luggage to purchase. Eddi didn't own the first garment carrier or overnight case. She'd never needed any. Again, Doug had insisted on buying only the best. She didn't want to know how much all this cost. She wondered if Mrs. Solange D'Martine would take one look at her and decide she'd wasted her money.

For the first time since she learned the truth about her conception, Eddi considered all that her mother had given up to protect her. She'd walked away from college to be a full-time mom and she'd turned her back on tremendous wealth because she feared for Eddi's safety. If her mother had chosen the more self-serving path, her entire life could have been different. Easier in many ways. But then, Eddi wouldn't have been blessed with the wonderful man she called Dad. And her mom would have missed out on sharing her life with a man who adored her.

Eddi blinked back a rush of tears. Everything happened for a reason. Though she wished things had turned out differently for Edouard D'Martine, she would never regret her life as it had been and was. Never.

"I need to spend some time with my mom and dad tonight." She met Doug's gaze when he glanced at her. "There are some things I need to say before I leave tomorrow."

"I understand."

A surge of affection welled inside her as she watched him for a long while after he turned his attention back to the road. He did understand and she was so thankful for his presence. Though she knew that he was being paid for his services, Eddi wanted to thank him personally. She hadn't decided how to do that yet. But she would.

Soon. Very soon.

EDDI SPENT THE REST of the afternoon and well into the evening with her parents. Doug stayed in the background, giving them all the space they needed. Saying goodbye, if only for a few days, was going to be tough for Eddi. She'd never been away from home for more than a night. But even a world traveler would have emotional misgivings in this instance.

The new world Eddi was about to venture into bore no resemblance whatsoever to the one in which she'd grown up. It was true that the coming change held numerous benefits, but Doug wasn't so sure the cost was worth it. Admittedly, he erred on the cynical side of the issue. His view was skewed. This was about Eddi, not him. She would do fine, he suspected. Besides, he had no part in the decision-making process. His sole responsibilities were to keep her safe from any and all threats and to facilitate the transition as he had today with the shopping spree.

She was a job…an assignment. He watched her share a final embrace with her parents before starting toward where he waited by the SUV. A job, he reminded himself as his eyes feasted on the way she moved…the fit of her jeans. A job, yes. And the most amazing woman he'd ever met.

"You're sure I can do this?" she asked as Doug pulled out on the street to drive her home. "I mean, what if I really screw up?"

"You'll do fine." He maneuvered a turn and flashed her a supportive smile. "I have complete confidence in you."

As was habit for her, she nibbled on her lower lip, making him want to touch her there and soothe the tortured flesh.

"I still don't get the fork thing," she said reflectively. "What if I use the salad fork for something other than the salad? They'll know how unrefined I am if I do that."

He cleared his throat to head off a chuckle. "Just start on the outside and work your way in. You can't go wrong. I'll be there, watch me if you get confused."

"Swear you won't leave my sight for an instant," she urged. "Swear it or I won't go."

He parked in her driveway and settled his gaze on hers, infusing all the assurance he could summon. "I won't let you out of my sight for a moment."

She exhaled a worried sigh. "Okay. As long as you're with me I can do this."

Ignoring the warning going off in his brain, he reached for her hand. Held it tenderly and reveled in the rush of desire that burned through him. "I'll be right there with you every step of the way."

Before he could fathom her intent, she leaned across the seat and kissed his cheek. In that infinitesimal moment before she drew away, it took every ounce of discipline he possessed not to kiss her back.

Not to draw her into his arms and kiss her the way she deserved to be kissed.

"Thank you," she murmured and hustled out of the vehicle before he could climb out and reach her door and open it for her. She didn't look at him as he approached. He felt sure she was embarrassed by her unexpected boldness and that only made her kiss all the more endearing.

"Uh-oh."

Doug followed her gaze to the yellow Cadillac parked half a block away. "Isn't that—"

"Yes," she hissed before he could finish the question.

Irene Marlowe, Ella Brown, Minnie and Mattie Caruthers marched up the sidewalk in their direction, arms loaded with items not readily identifiable. All looked prepared to fight some sort of battle. A twinge of apprehension went through Doug. This couldn't be good.

"Ms. Irene, Ms. Ella." Eddi looked from one to the next. "Ms. Minnie. Ms. Mattie. What's going on?"

"We've reached a decision," Ms. Ella said solemnly.

"Oh, yes." Minnie picked up where she left off. "We've spent the entire day talking about it."

Doug's apprehension escalated, sending his pulse into hyper mode.

"And we've determined that an intervention is in order," Mattie summed up.

The frown currently distorting Eddi's lovely features no doubt matched Doug's own. What the hell were these women talking about? Then he got a closer look at the articles they held in their arms, videos with titles that could only be X-rated. Several risqué magazines, the kind he'd sneaked peeks at back in junior high school. What in blazes was this about?

"Intervention?" Eddi asked, her tone uncertain.

Irene nodded firmly. "Mr. Douglas Cooper is the one. We're sure of it. Our cause shall not be averted simply because he has chosen the wrong path. We believe there's hope." She winked and tapped the quart-size mason jar she carried. "And just in case he needs some loosening up, we brought along a little Remedy as well."

Now he was really worried. He'd wager this had something to do with last night and their scheming to find a mate for Eddi.

"What're you talking about?" Eddi prodded warily. "What do you mean the one? What wrong path?"

Mattie jostled her videos to one arm and planted her free hand on her hip. "Why, the one for you, of course. We're not going to let a simple thing like his being gay stop us."

Doug tensed inwardly. This was worse than he'd thought.

"What?" Eddi demanded, clearly as frustrated and concerned as he was.

"We've devised a cure," Irene said with a look of sympathy in Doug's direction. "Now, there's no time to waste. Let's go inside and get started."

"Ladies," Doug admonished gently. "I'm afraid there's been some misunderstanding."

"Let me explain," Eddi offered with a reassuring hand on his arm. "This is my fault anyway."

Doug acquiesced to her lead and ordered his runaway libido not to overreact to her simple touch. His order was promptly overruled.

"Come on inside, ladies," Eddi offered, waving the group toward her door. "There's something I need to tell you."

Thirty minutes later, with coffee served all around, and the ladies squeezed together on the sofa, all stared agog at Eddi as she finished her story.

For several moments no one said anything. Doug resisted the urge to reach across the small table that separated them and take Eddi's hand. She badly needed the support of her friends right now.

"So." Ms. Irene was the first to recover. "You're an heir to the D'Martine fortune?"

Eddi nodded.

Irene's hand flew to her throat. "Well, that certainly explains a lot of things."

Eddi frowned. "What do you mean?"

Irene smiled knowingly. "Honey, I always knew there was something special about you. I just couldn't put my finger on what it was. The way you help people…work for free more often than not when someone is in need. Knowing full well you're in need most of the time yourself. The D'Martines have always been generous with their wealth."

Eddi gasped. "You know them?"

Irene inclined her head toward one shoulder in a hint of a shrug. "I know of them. The family used to make headlines all the time."

"And your father has known all along?" Ella wanted to know.

"Yes." Eddi added quickly, "But he loved me and raised me just like his own."

"Well, of course he did," Minnie charged. "I've never known a man who loved his family more." She fanned herself with her handkerchief. "What a story, my dear!"

"You've all got to promise that you'll keep my secret a while." She glanced at Doug. "There are things I have to do before this thing goes public."

"We understand," Ella assured. The other three ladies nodded their concurrence.

"I knew I was right about him from the beginning," Mattie piped up, tossing Doug a knowing look. "I said he was a spy and I was close."

"He's a bodyguard," Irene protested irritably. "Not a spy, Mattie. There's a difference."

Mattie pooh-poohed the comment with a wave of her hands. "Spy, bodyguard, whatever. I never believed he was gay for a second. No man who was gay would look at our Eddi the way I've seen this young fellow looking at her. Why, I'd bet he's—"

"More coffee, anyone?" Doug asked, cutting her off before she could get him in any deeper. It was time for an intervention of his own. One that included getting Meadowbrook's matchmakers out the door.

The last thing he needed was Eddi taking note of his mistake. Bodyguards weren't supposed to lust after their charges.

Her startled look in his direction told him he was already too late.

Chapter Eight

By noon on Sunday they had arrived at a small airfield aboard the D'Martine private jet, rented a car and driven to Woods Hole where they caught the ferry to Martha's Vineyard.

Eddi had never seen anyplace more beautiful in her life. Roughly shaped like a triangle, the island's coastline defied adequate description, with its sand dunes and beach grasses and craggy cliffs, it personified rugged beauty. The view of the white sandy beaches and scattering of summerhouses was nothing short of breathtaking. The homes ranged from gingerbread cottages to large estates. Some, according to Doug, were lived in full-time, but most were summer homes.

After the ferry docked and while Eddi waited for Doug to see to the unloading of the rental car, she inhaled the sharp scent of salt air and coastal vegetation. The breeze and sun were warm against her skin and the call of birds helped to ease the agitation that had been building since she boarded that plane this morning.

Her parents hadn't come to the airport to see her off, which was good. It would have proven too emotional and she hadn't needed that. Bolstering her courage to take her first-ever flight was tough enough. But Doug had been right beside her, just as he'd promised. He'd talked her through the rocky parts and made her laugh too many times to recall.

She watched him now and smiled. Though clearly he was not used to handling a group of meddling old ladies like the members of the Club, he managed to roll with the punches exceptionally well. Eddi was convinced that all four of the ladies were infatuated with him already. And they weren't alone. She blinked and looked away. This was business for him. She had to stop letting those foolish thoughts surface. Just because Ms. Irene and her crew thought he was "the one" for her, didn't mean he was. Eddi felt confident that he merely tolerated them all for the sake of the job and would have a good laugh when his assignment was over.

Eddi's chest constricted painfully when she thought of his leaving. Boy, was she in a pickle. She didn't know how in the world she was going to get over losing the man when he'd never even been hers.

The drive to Chilmark, the small town where the D'Martine estate was located, went a long way in keeping Eddi's mind off her troubles. Rolling hills and gorgeous coastline were only the beginning. The landscape unfolded like that of a fairy tale. Stone fences and sheep farms ribboned the hills. A lovely old church and village school marked the center of town as they passed through it. The farms and fishing villages they encountered along the countryside were spectacular, but it was the coastline, bar none, that made this part of the island magnificent. Elegant private yachts lay along the docks side by side with draggers and the more rustic vessels of lobstermen.

Just when she was certain nothing she could see would prove more beautiful, Doug took a right and drove up a winding road that led to the D'Martine estate. The house had the look of an English manor and it sat high on a bluff overlooking the Atlantic Ocean. Surrounded on three sides by acres and acres of forests and then encircled more intimately by a wrought-iron security fence, the mansion definitely dwarfed into insignificance all else she had seen.

Doug entered the code, which had been provided to him by Mr. Thurston, and the forbidding security gates opened wide for them to enter.

"Holy smokes," Eddi murmured.

"Remember," Doug said, drawing her attention to him as he slowly rolled up the cobblestone driveway, "it's only a house, just like yours back home."

"Only bigger," she breathed, her gaze swinging back to the house that loomed before them. *"A whole lot bigger."*

He parked in front of the house and hesitated before getting out. "The people inside, Eddi, are only people. Keep that in mind. Okay?"

She nodded, too mesmerized by all that she saw to bother with words. This was where Edouard had been born and raised. Her heart was suddenly beating too fast and Eddi felt the overwhelming urge to demand that Doug take her back home. What was she doing here? She didn't belong here. This wasn't who Eddi Harper was.

Before she could make those very observations out loud, Doug was out of the car and opening her door.

As Eddi emerged, the massive front door opened and a tall, well-dressed man, probably in his late sixties, descended the steps, paused at the bottom and executed a sort of bow for her.

"Miss Harper," he said in a voice that was both refined and perfectly modulated, "we've been expecting you."

"Douglas Cooper," Doug said, taking the pressure of a response from Eddi.

The man acknowledged his introduction with a nod. "James Montgomery. Someone will see to your car, Mr. Cooper. Now, if you don't mind, Mrs. D'Martine and Mr. Thurston are waiting."

Mr. Montgomery promptly turned on his heel and led the way up the steps. Doug leaned down and whispered, "The butler."

Eddi absorbed the information and chastised herself for not thinking of that. A house this size and a family this wealthy would have a full household staff. Maids, cooks, butler, the works.

Inside, Eddi barely covered her mouth before a gasp escaped. The foyer was incredible and huge! Marble floors and paneled walls. A double, sweeping staircase unfolded like welcoming arms and flowed onto a second-story landing. It rivaled any other she'd seen in the movies or in magazines. Vases of fresh flowers sat here and there and exquisite artwork adorned the walls. But the one thing that made her pulse skip was the huge family portrait that hung on the wall midway up one side of the staircase. Directly across on the opposite side a grouping of smaller, individual portraits hung, but it was the massive one that mesmerized her.

Before she could study the details more closely, Mr. Montgomery paused near a closed set of rich mahogany double doors. "I'll be along with tea, sir. Please join Mrs. D'Martine in the library."

"Thank you, Montgomery," Doug said in a tone that was every bit as refined as the butler's. Without further explanation he opened the doors and stood back for Eddi to enter before him.

Had Doug been here before? Or were all mansions built on the same floor plan? He sure seemed to know all the right moves.

The library turned out to be a cross between an office and a den…only bigger than any she'd ever seen.

Mr. Thurston stood near a grand fireplace that dominated the far wall.

"Ah, Miss Harper, Mr. Cooper, you've arrived."

Well, duh, Eddi mused. Why was it everyone around here liked to state the obvious?

"Mr. Thurston," Doug said without offering his hand this time.

Eddi was pretty sure she'd picked up on some bad vibes between the two men when she first met them. Doug didn't appear to like Mr. High-and-Mighty Attorney.

"Edwinna."

Eddi looked up at the sound of her name. A woman stood next to Mr. Thurston now. She'd evidently been seated in the high wingback chair facing the fireplace and keeping her hidden from view. But Eddi could see her now. Her breath hitched again as her eyes took in what her brain was so slow to accept. The woman standing only a few feet away was maybe in her seventies, but still looked fit. She was of average height and rather thin. Her manner of dress was impeccable. But none of that was responsible for Eddi's runaway pulse. The woman looked so very much like Eddi, only older. Pictures just didn't provide the full impact. A small shock rocked through her and she had to close her eyes then look again to be sure she wasn't imagining things.

"Dear God," the older woman murmured. "She is just as you described, Brandon."

The attorney nodded, then said to Eddi, "Miss Harper, may I present to you your grandmother, Solange D'Martine."

When Eddi stood there, rooted to the spot, Solange took the initiative and moved toward her.

"Thank you for coming, Edwinna." She smiled and took Eddi by the arms just long enough to press one cheek to hers. "I am so happy to have you home," she added when she drew away.

"Eddi," she insisted tightly. "Call me Eddi." The heart that only moments ago had been racing now flopped jerkily in her chest.

Solange acknowledged the request with a vague smile. "I hope your trip was pleasant."

"Yes. It was fine," Eddi assured her. What did she say now? She prayed Doug would rescue her.

Thankfully he didn't have to. The doors opened and the butler entered carrying a tray. Without a word, he placed it on a nearby table, executed another of those small bows in Solange's direction and made his exit as efficiently as he'd entered.

"Shall we sit?" Solange suggested in a voice that still held just the slightest glimmer of a European accent. "I'm sure you're exhausted and in need of refreshment."

Eddi was more than certain that she could not drink anything at the moment. Her stomach was tied in a thousand knots. It took all her resolve not to wring her hands. Trying not to stumble over Doug who, thankfully, prepared to sit beside her on the sofa, she could scarcely take her eyes off her grandmother.

Solange had the same strawberry-blond hair, though it was mostly gray now, and the streak of pure white was exactly like Eddi's. And the eyes...sweet Jesus...the blue eyes were duplicates of her own.

Solange settled in an elegantly tufted satin chair and studied Eddi with the same curiosity. Finally, she said, "I've considered at length where we should start and I believe that it is in our best interests to speak openly and honestly."

Eddi nodded her agreement, then shook her head at the attorney when he offered her a cup of tea. Totally at ease in the environment, Doug accepted the offer of refreshment, which postponed the conversation a few seconds. Eddi tried to calm herself...to slow her respiration, but her efforts were useless.

"You are the daughter of my one and only son, part of his flesh, his blood flows through your veins," Solange announced quietly and determinedly. "That alone makes you more valuable to me than anything else on earth."

Eddi swallowed or attempted to. Emotion had closed her throat, but she managed a jerky nod. A verbal response was out of the question.

"My only request is that we take the next few days and get to know each other and then you can make a decision as to whether you would choose to accept what is rightfully yours.''

''I don't understand.'' Eddi shook her head. ''What is it that you believe is rightfully mine?''

Solange D'Martine focused that eerily familiar blue gaze on Eddi's and said without hesitation, ''All that I possess.''

''SHE CAN'T BE SERIOUS!''

Doug waited patiently for Eddi to calm down, but it didn't appear that was going to happen in the near future. She paced the lavish room she'd been provided like a caged lion.

''I mean, I know I'm the only heir and that she doesn't have anyone else, but, jeepers, why would she say such a thing? She doesn't even know me. I could be some sort of con artist. Well, she did have me investigated, I imagine.''

''Is that a rhetorical question?'' Doug mused. He smiled in consolation. ''After all, you did answer the question even before you asked it.''

She wheeled on him, shooting daggers at him with those sea-blue eyes. ''You know what I mean.''

He knew a number of things. Like the fact that the soft pink slacks and matching sweater looked fantastic on her. Anyone who wondered if there had been a womanly figure hidden under those overalls wouldn't have any questions now. Womanly and enticing. He resisted the urge to shake his head at his poor judgment and total lack of discipline. Keeping his perspective was supposed to be easier now.

She spun around and paced the length of the room again, giving him a gut-wrenching view of her very,

very fine derriere. Not only had those overalls been hiding her figure, they had, apparently, camouflaged her ability to walk like a temptress. How could anyone so innocent move so sensually?

The precise reason he shouldn't be having these thoughts, he reminded the part of him that refused to see reason.

"What am I supposed to do with all this?" She waved her arms magnanimously. "I'm a plumber, not a...a whatever she is."

"Eddi, don't get so bent out of shape just yet," he suggested in a far calmer tone than he had justification to possess at the moment. "Do as Mrs. D'Martine suggested. Take a few days. See what she's offering and then make your decision."

"You're no help!" She puffed out a frustrated breath. "You sound just like them."

A new kind of tension slid through him. Time to shift gears a bit. He stood and joined her in the center of the room where she momentarily hovered, looking ready to burst into tears or to start stamping her foot in frustration.

"Listen to me," he suggested gently. "Solange is agoraphobic. She never leaves the house. I'm certain she fears for the empire her husband's family spent generations building. Admittedly she has a loyal board of directors and a top-notch CEO, but that's not quite the same as having the personal touch from a true member of the family. I'm thinking that she desperately wants you to take up where your ancestors left off. In her eyes, it's your birthright...your duty."

"Ohhh." Eddi took her head in her hands. "But I don't need another duty. I told you that before."

"You also told me," he reminded a tad more firmly, "that you wanted to help your *real* family."

She made a weary sound and wrapped her arms around her middle. "I do. But..." She shook her head. "This is all too overwhelming. How can I make a decision when there's so much to consider. I don't know anything about any of this."

He smiled down at her and wished he could take her in his arms and comfort her the way he longed to. "You'll know all you need to in a few days. Trust yourself, Eddi. You'll make the right decision."

Before he realized her intention, she leaned into him. Rested her forehead against his chest. Doug told himself not to move...not to respond, but he couldn't help himself. His arms went around her.

"I'm afraid," she murmured into his shirt. She knotted her fingers there and moved in closer, aligning her body with his until he thought he would groan with the pleasure of it.

"What are you afraid of?" he whispered, his lips nestled against her sweet-smelling hair.

"I'm afraid I'll lose myself."

Doug understood exactly how she felt. There had been a time not so long ago that he'd lost himself. No one who hadn't been there could possibly understand just how frightening the prospect was. For that reason, and that reason alone, he held her. Held her until she felt strong enough to stand on her own again. Held her closer than he'd ever held anyone else before, until she was ready to let go.

DOWNSTAIRS, JUST BEFORE dinner, Eddi was introduced to a dozen members of the household staff, including maids, cooks, gardeners and her grandmother D'Martine's private secretary who had come for dinner just to meet Eddi.

As Doug had promised, he stayed close by. Eddi looked to his lead for each course that was served. He never let her down, not once. Warmth spread like wildfire through her each time she thought of the tender way he'd held her this evening when she'd all but come undone. He'd held her for as long as she needed him to and not for a second had he allowed it to turn sexual. He just held her until her fears passed.

Not that she was no longer afraid, but she did feel more prepared to face what lay ahead of her.

Since he occupied the room directly across the hall from hers, she felt comfortable and safe. At least as safe and comfortable as she could this far away from home.

A stab of homesickness plunged deep into her chest when she thought of her parents and how worried they were. They tried to hide it, but she knew. She'd called to let them know she had arrived safely and she could hear the worry in her mother's voice. This was so hard on them.

And she didn't want that.

Realizing her grandmother was speaking to her, Eddi jerked back to the present. She mentally scrambled to catch up with the conversation.

"You've had a lot with which to cope today, I'm certain," Solange was saying. "Taking that into consideration, we won't make any plans for this evening. But tomorrow I'd like to begin your proper introduction to the family history and all that your birthright entails.''

Uncertain of herself even to make an appropriate response, Eddi looked to Doug. He nodded once, giving her the go-ahead. Her courage bolstered, she smiled and replied, ''I'd like that.''

Her response appeared to please Solange thus providing Eddi with serious relief. She scanned those seated at the enormous dining table and wondered if they ever looked around and asked themselves how it was possible for one person to have amassed such wealth.

Eddi supposed not. Thurston and the others were likely used to this sort of thing. They would consider her life back home in Meadowbrook meager and meaningless. Doubt twisted inside Eddi once more. Of course, she found all of this incredibly exciting on one level, but the fear she had shared with Doug haunted her on a dozen others. What if she allowed herself to be lured into this world of glamour and glitz? There would be no room for the Eddi she had always been.

She had to hold on with both hands and pray that insignificant little Edwinna Harper, plumber extraordinaire, didn't get lost in the shuffle. She glanced around the elaborately decorated and furnished room that was larger than her whole house. Getting lost in all this would be far too easy. Her gaze sought Doug. He was her anchor. Her rock. All that kept her steady. She could count on Doug.

DOUG SHOULDERED OUT OF his holster and weapon and tossed both onto the bed. He hoped he wouldn't have to use excessive force in this assignment. He didn't want to think about Eddi being caught in the line of fire. Now or ever. But the precaution was, unfortunately, necessary considering the tragic D'Martine history.

Solange D'Martine was one determined woman. She made no bones about her intentions. She fully anticipated Eddi's becoming an integral part of her family as well as her business dealings. If Doug had his guess, she'd expected to do that even before meeting Eddi. The whole situation definitely warranted the feelings of being overwhelmed that Eddi suffered.

Eddi was caught between the love for the parents who'd raised her and the desire to learn about her biological father and the heritage he had left her. Right now Eddi didn't want to admit any such desire, but it was there. Doug could feel it. She wanted to know...to be a part of it on some level. But her loyalty to Millicent and Harvey Harper would hold her back.

Not for long, Doug would wager. Eddi, like her grandmother, was far too determined to pretend away all that had been offered to her. Conversely, Doug didn't doubt for a second that she would always take care of her parents. But this was bigger than her and it had already done a hell of a job of swallowing her up. She simply hadn't owned up to it just yet.

Doug could only hope she would have the required tough exterior to handle one of the less-than-pleasant aspects of wealth and instant fame— the media. She would learn very soon how cruel the wielders of the mighty pen could be.

He couldn't protect her fully from that, but he'd

try to prepare her for it. That way it wouldn't come as such a shock. They had talked about the various celebrities who had been hounded by the press in recent years. The Duchess of York, the late Princess Diana, the Kennedy children.

Readers thrived on learning what the rich and famous were up to. Doug didn't really have a problem with that. What annoyed him was the false reporting. The kind of reporting that had lost him the one woman he'd loved in this lifetime.

His playboy reputation, which was grossly overstated, and the fact that he was the last male member of the Cooper-Smith family who wasn't wed, had been played to the hilt. When his fiancée could handle the innuendos no longer, she'd dumped him and walked away without looking back once. His whole world had been shattered. For the first time in his life, Doug had realized he didn't even know who he was. He worked in his father's Wall Street office. He played in the same social circles as his siblings and he did all the things expected of him. Attended the right school, dated the proper female candidates. He focused so completely on doing everything right, he forgot one important thing—himself.

When his fiancée rocked his world by walking out, he realized that he didn't even know who he was. Never had, not really. So the journey had begun. To his family's dismay, he bowed out of the limelight and devoted himself to a smaller part in the world. One which allowed him to feel as if what he did really mattered in the final scheme of things. Slowly but surely he'd found the man he wanted to be.

This—he looked around the lavish room—was no longer the place for him.

A light rap on his door dragged his attention back to the present. He knew by the hesitation and lack of authority behind the soft knock that it was Eddi. That aside, all it took was one glance at the small monitor positioned next to his bed to know she'd left her room. He quickly turned the monitor off since he wasn't sure Eddi would approve of her grandmother's security measures.

When he opened the door she stared up at him, already dressed in her lovely new silk negligee, and blurted, "I can't sleep. Do you mind if I hang out with you a while?"

Doug told himself not to but his eyes appeared to have a mind of their own. He slowly, thoroughly surveyed every single detail of how the peach-colored silk lay against her skin.

"Yeah, sure," he said at last when he'd stared as long as politely possible. It was a mistake, but he stepped aside and allowed her to enter his room, the silk whispering against her flesh as she moved.

For a while she simply stood there in the center of his room. She declined to sit when he offered and insisted she wanted nothing to drink. But, she wanted something, that much was clear. His entire body reacted to her presence...to the unspoken need emanating from her.

Finally, she looked up at him and said the last thing he'd expected to hear, "Doug, I know this is above and beyond the call of duty, but would you mind kissing me?"

One eyebrow tilted upward. "Kiss you?" Anticipation roared through him. This was not a good idea. But, damn, if he didn't want to.

She nodded. "I don't think I'll make it through the night if I don't get my mind off—" she flung her arms open wide "—all this. I need something else to focus on. I figure a kiss would do it." She stared at the floor but not before he saw the beginnings of a blush creeping up her cheeks. "I'll never go to sleep if I don't find something else to dwell on."

If she hadn't looked so damn needy or so absolutely vulnerable, he might have been able to say no. But, there was simply no way he could deny her anything, least of all a kiss.

"Come here," he demanded softly.

Stealing a glance up at him as she tortured that gorgeous bottom lip, she took a halting step toward him and then another and another until she stood directly in front of him.

"You don't mind?" she whispered, looking fiercely uncertain and undeniably sexy.

"Shh," he scolded as his mouth descended toward hers.

Her breath caught when their lips met. Doug hesitated, waited to see if she'd changed her mind. Two seconds later she took a hesitant taste of him. So soft, so uncertain. So damn sweet. He struggled to hold back the need mushrooming out of control and forced himself to remain still, letting her do what she would. She kissed him experimentally at first, then tiptoed to kiss him more aggressively. Her fingers fisted in his shirt and control snapped.

He plunged his fingers into her hair and angled her head just the right way so that he could kiss her thoroughly. She tasted rich and sweet, like the wine they'd drank at dinner. Desire coiled more deeply inside him, threatening to burst and push him completely over the edge. She moaned softly, opened her mouth to him and he thrust inside, ravenous for the full taste of her. Not until that moment had he confessed just how much he wanted her. He wanted to know all of her.

But a kiss was all this could be.

She melted against him, all soft curves and feminine heat. His body hardened instantly, sharpening the demand for more.

He drew back, his breath ragged. If he didn't stop now there would be no stopping.

"Enough?"

Her lids fluttered open and she looked at him through dazed eyes. "No…yes…I…"

"Good night, Eddi." He ushered her to the door. "Tomorrow's going to be a long day."

She nodded and padded across the hall to her own room. He watched her go, gripping the door frame to keep from following her. She paused at her door and smiled at him. "Good night." Then she was gone.

Doug sighed. There was no chance in hell he would have a good night. A long night, yes, but definitely not a good night.

Chapter Nine

It was the curse.

Eddi was sure of it. The matchmaking members of the Club had put the idea in her head and she was subconsciously acting on it.

That's all it could be.

Why else would she have done something so incredibly stupid last night? She'd practically begged the guy to kiss her.

Eddi groaned and collapsed onto the bed. She had lost her mind. It was official. All the years of financial worry and hard work were finally catching up to her at the ripe old age of twenty-five minus a few days. Of course it didn't help that her whole life had been turned upside down by an old family secret.

Temporary insanity. That's what she'd plead. She would explain to Doug that she'd snapped, lost it, and he would understand. After all, he knew what she'd been through the past few days. Who wouldn't have snapped? Anyone else would have reacted the same way.

She closed her eyes and tried without much success to block the memories of his utterly amazing kiss.

Never in a million years would she have imagined a kiss that pulse pounding, knee weakening was possible. He'd kissed her tenderly at first, then his attention had turned possessive and fierce. A moment's fear had claimed her but that sensation had swiftly sizzled into flat-out, core-melting desire.

All she'd wanted was a distraction…something to take her mind off her surroundings. What she'd gotten had been just another worry to add to the growing list. No, that first part wasn't right. She'd wanted more than a distraction. She wanted him to kiss her so that the spell would be broken. Her momma had always told her that most folks spent the better part of their lives wanting what they couldn't have. The longer one dwelled on it, the more attractive it became. She'd figured that was the case with her growing attachment to Doug. She knew he would never be hers…that no sort of relationship would be possible between a world-wise man like him and a plain Jane like her. So she'd decided to nip the situation in the bud. All she had to do was prove to herself that he was just a guy and that his kiss wouldn't be any better than any other she'd ever had. Not that she'd had that many.

Boy, had she ever been wrong.

Now she was doomed to live with the truth—Doug Cooper was one heck of a kisser and definitely "the one" for her. She didn't need the matchmakers here to tell her; she'd felt it all the way to her bones. She was in love with the guy. One kiss was all it had taken.

Lord have mercy, she'd used the "L" word.

What a mess.

A light tap echoed from her closed bedroom door. Her breath trapped in her throat.

"Miss Harper?"

James, the butler, she recognized. Forcing thoughts of her pitiful love life to the back of her mind, she shoved off the bed and strode to the door. She incorporated the walk Doug had told her about. Shoulders back, chin held high, but the high-heeled pumps made her a bit unsteady. She wished again for her sneakers. Dress shoes were for one thing only, wearing to church on Sunday. She had decided long ago that the discomfort served as her penance for whatever bad thought she'd allowed that week.

Today she would wear them to remind her of the foolhardy thing she'd done last night.

The very idea that a big-city guy like Doug would take even a second look at a blue-collar girl like her... Talk about fairy tales. Guys simply didn't look at her that way.

Eddi opened the door and produced a smile for the elegantly dressed man who waited on the other side of her door.

"Good morning, Miss Harper." He nodded once in acknowledgment of her smile. "I've brought your coffee and toast up as Mrs. D'Martine requested."

A frown crinkled Eddi's forehead. "Is there some reason she wanted me to be served in my room?" Maybe she had company this morning and wasn't ready for Eddi to be seen.

James smiled. "No, madam. Mrs. D'Martine doesn't breakfast until eight o'clock. She didn't want you to have to wait."

It was seven now. She could have waited. But, he

was here. Might as well make the best of it. She certainly didn't want to hurt feelings or offend anyone. She did wonder though how her grandmother knew she was an early riser. "Sure. Okay. Come in."

James entered the room, his back ramrod straight, and crossed to the sitting area. After placing the tray on the table he faced her once more. "Is there anything else that would pleasure you this morning, miss?"

Eddi clasped her hands behind her back and strolled over to the table. She dismissed the idea of telling him the guy across the hall could definitely pleasure her. "Do you mind answering a few questions for me?"

His expression never deviated from its emotionless state. "If I can, I will be quite happy to."

She circled the table and studied the bounty he'd delivered on a silver tray. The toast was browned to perfection. Softened butter sat nearby. A small jar of blueberry jam completed the menu. The matching silver coffeepot looked just large enough to hold two cups of coffee. Cream and sugar were artfully arranged nearby.

She poured herself a cup of the steaming brew and sat down in one of the two chairs flanking the table. "Are you allowed to sit while we talk?"

"Certainly." He settled into the adjacent chair as gracefully as a ballerina executing a dance move and with every bit as much pomp and circumstance.

James Montgomery had gray hair and gray eyes. He stood tall and thin and looked friendly, in a vague sort of way. She liked him.

"How long have you worked with the D'Martine

family?'' Couldn't hurt to know some background. She had an hour. She probably didn't need to spend any more time alone with Doug, and she definitely didn't need to obsess on that unforgettable kiss.

''Thirty-five years.'' His chest seemed to puff with pride to punctuate his words.

''So you knew my—Edouard.''

''I did.'' His gaze roamed her face then. ''If I may, you are assuredly his daughter. The resemblance is remarkable.''

Something like pride welled in Eddi's chest then and she hadn't even known Edouard. But somehow she knew that if her mother had loved him he must have been a very special man.

''What was he like?'' A prickle of apprehension needled her. She hadn't meant to ask that. But there it was all the same.

''A very fine, passionate young man.'' A glimmer of sadness showed briefly in the other man's expression. ''He is still sorely missed.''

''Mrs. D'Martine—'' Eddi swallowed and rephrased her question, ''My grandmother never leaves the house?''

James shook his head, his expression openly grim now. ''She has not left this house since her husband was buried only weeks after Edouard.''

Eddi thought of the woman she had met just yesterday. How sad that her life had been stolen also. She'd lost all that she loved within a matter of weeks and then she'd turned her back on life as well.

What kept her going in spite of her losses? That was something Eddi longed to know. For Eddi's mother, it had been her child and the love of a good man. But Solange D'Martine had had neither.

"Is there anything that has made her happy even once in all these years?"

"Her devotion to keeping the family business alive and growing has kept her passion for life alive…just barely. But only one thing has truly made her happy in the past twenty-five years," James said, his expression unreadable once more.

So there was something in her life that kept her going besides work. "What's that?" Eddi had to know, had to understand a little more about her grandmother.

James stood and for one second Eddi thought he would leave without answering her question, then his somber gray gaze settled onto hers. "Why, you, miss. *You.*"

ONCE THE BUTLER HAD LEFT Eddi's room, Doug walked across the hall and rapped on her closed door. He didn't look forward to facing her this morning. He'd lost control for a moment last night and that couldn't happen twice. No matter that kissing her a second time now held the top spot on his list of things he had to do again before dying.

His integrity had slipped and he could not permit such behavior. He wasn't about to do anything that would screw up his new life. Or hers.

The door swung inward and Eddi stood there, dressed in the emerald-green skirt and sweater that both fit like a glove and complemented her pale coloring.

"Good morning," he said in the most professional manner he could summon while looking at her.

She nodded mutely. Only then did he notice that she looked ready to burst into tears.

"Is something wrong?" Had Montgomery, the butler, passed along some disconcerting message? Or had the man said something inappropriate to Eddi. Doug had fully expected some animosity toward her from those who'd served Mrs. D'Martine the longest. They would see Eddi as an outsider, a gold digger.

She shook her head and shrugged at the same time. "I don't know." With a beleaguered sigh and some rapid blinking she appeared to get her emotions under control. Leaving the door open for him to follow if he chose, she trudged across the room and dropped into a chair. "This is going to be complicated," she muttered and promptly plopped her chin into her hand.

It was definitely going to be that.

In more ways than one. Already his pulse had tripped into double time simply being alone in the room with her.

"Would you like to take a walk?"

Her expression lifted instantly. "Yes!"

THE GROUNDS OF THE D'Martine estate proved as tranquil as they were beautiful. So much so that even the beefed-up security measures did not detract from its appeal. Doug had spent most every summer of his life on the island since his family owned a summerhouse in Tisbury. Not unlike the D'Martine property, the Cooper-Smith compound projected a look and feel of luxury, only in a more understated and contemporary manner.

"This place is unbelievable," Eddi said again. "Keeping those gardens in shape must require an entire staff of gardeners."

"Probably," Doug agreed. The gardens of which she spoke were close reproductions of the distinguished ones he'd been exposed to as a boy on one of his mother's numerous trips abroad, specifically to England and France.

In fact, the whole estate had a very European feel, from the architecture to the landscaping. The salt air and crash of the waves on the sand below only added another layer of elegance to the ambience. He imagined that bringing a touch of home, of old-world flavor, had been the D'Martine's intent.

Eddi stopped and stared out over the blue waters of the Atlantic. She said nothing for a long while, but Doug sensed that something specific was on her mind.

"She's not going to expect me to live here, is she?" The gaze that very closely resembled the color of the foaming water locked with his. "It's a truly beautiful place, but this isn't my home. How could I stay?"

Doug wanted to reassure her, to allay her worries on that point, but anything he said might prove wrong in the end. "Eddi, this is your home now," he said frankly. When she would have argued, he added, "It won't replace the one back in Meadowbrook, but it will become a part of your life."

Already her life was changing and she wasn't even aware of it. He had observed little things. Like the extra trouble she'd taken to add a jeweled clip to her long hair. The hint of extravagant cologne on her skin. She might not understand what was happening, but it *was* happening.

She looked away then. "I didn't ask for this."

The words were spoken so softly he scarcely heard them.

"I know." An ache throbbed through him so deeply that it took his breath for a moment. He simply could not stand there and allow her to suffer this burden alone. He draped one arm around her shoulders and gave her a comforting squeeze. "But fate has a way of carving out our destiny even when we don't want it to."

For a very long time they stood there, watching the waves roll to the shore and foam on the sand. The crisp breeze and the occasional seagull flying overhead was all that moved above the surface of the water. They could have been standing on a deserted island. Doug had never felt more connected to anyone in his life.

Eddi was right, things were very complicated, and only growing more so by the moment.

EDDI STOOD OUTSIDE HER grandmother D'Martine's private suite for as long as she dared before knocking and then opening the door. She'd tried to pull herself together, to tamp down the anxiety skyrocketing inside her. But it was just no use.

"Please join me," Solange requested with a wave of her hand toward the sofa next to her.

Her feet aching after the long walk around the estate, Eddi just did manage to cross the room without a noticeable limp. Propping a smile into place, she settled next to her grandmother. Her gaze went immediately to the table before them and the numerous photo albums piled there.

"I wanted to introduce you to your father."

Eddi didn't bother correcting her, she knew what she meant. Instead, she brightened her smile and said, "I'd like that." And she would to an extent. This was an important part of who she was, or so it seemed, and she needed as much background information as possible. "I have some pictures to share with you, too."

For the next two hours, Solange D'Martine led Eddi on a journey through time. Just over fifty years ago a beautiful child had been born to a couple who had only recently settled in this country. Hailing from France, the D'Martines had decided that they wanted to live in America. To bear and raise their children here. They had purchased this estate the moment they laid eyes on it since it reminded them so very much of home with its European flair and setting.

Edouard had been a joy as a child. Beautiful and gregarious. He lacked for nothing while growing up and in return he served the family business well, including working toward a degree in contract law. He was to be in charge one day and since he remained an only child, he was everything to his parents. Eddi shared the photo album of her childhood her mother had prepared with Solange.

"I had no idea he'd met someone," Solange said as she studied the pictures of Edouard with Eddi's mother. Eddi's chest ached as she shuffled through the loose stack of photographs that belonged to her grandmother.

"Where did you get these pictures?" If her mother and Edouard's relationship had been secret, where had the pictures come from?

"They were among his things in Boston. He had a small apartment there for facilitating his attendance at the university."

God, her mother looked so young...and so happy. And Edouard, well, he was just about the handsomest man she'd ever seen. Guilt immediately nudged her. Besides her dad, she amended.

"I had no idea who she was and, quite honestly, I was too grief stricken to pursue any such matters. It was months before I accidentally discovered the pictures. By then your mother had disappeared."

"They were really in love," Eddi said more to herself than to Solange.

"Very much so."

Eddi looked up at the sound of pain in her grandmother's voice.

"If he had only trusted me perhaps this horrible thing would not have happened."

Unable to help herself, Eddi placed a hand atop her grandmother's. She looked so forlorn, so stricken, Eddi ached for her. "What do you mean?" she asked, not certain she really wanted to know but unable to ignore the statement.

"If he had told me of his love for your mother then there would have been no need for such secretive rendezvous and perhaps he would have been here with her, instead of in some small flat in the unsavory part of a town many miles away."

Her mother had told her that Edouard feared telling

his parents about their relationship. "It wasn't your fault," she felt compelled to say.

The pain etched on her face deepened. "Yes, it was. We were so hard on him, expected so very much of him. When he found true love with a woman of so little means he feared we would forbid such a match."

Eddi's heart thundered in her ears. She had to know the rest of it. "Would you have forbidden the relationship?"

Her gaze bright with emotion, Solange shook her head sadly. "That is the worst tragedy of all. Your father never knew that his father had chosen likewise." She drew in a heavy breath. "My family was very poor. We had nothing. But we never told Edouard. Since my parents were long dead when he was born, there was no reason to bring it up. I had no other close family. It simply had no bearing on our lives. Such things were not discussed." She shook her head slowly from side to side. "Who would have guessed that keeping such a secret would carry such a high price?"

Eddi squeezed her hand. "You can't be sure his knowing that secret would have made a difference. You didn't do anything wrong. Some evil man or men did this, not you. Surely you know that?"

She managed a watery smile. "I tell myself that every day." She took Eddi's hand in both of hers. "But you are here now. God has not forsaken me altogether. For that, I am very grateful."

Summoning her courage, Eddi asked, "How did you find me?"

Solange looked distant a moment. "Quite by accident. James was visiting a cousin in Maryland and he saw you.'' She shook her head. ''He was beside himself until we'd verified who you are.'' Her gaze settled heavily onto Eddi's. ''We're a close group…we've all anticipated your arrival.''

Eddi was almost relieved when they moved on to the subject of the D'Martine jewelry business. Her emotions were raw. She wasn't sure she could get through much more of this intense bonding. She watched her grandmother, a woman at once sophisticated and simple. Though Solange D'Martine bore the classic characteristics of a very sophisticated woman in every respect, personal as well as professional, she remained open and honest, simple in a way that demanded respect.

The bottom line was, Solange D'Martine was a woman without a fancy education, without an idyllic childhood, and still she commanded respect and admiration. She was a woman with an agenda who would not be defeated. The realization galvanized the emotions whirling inside Eddi.

Not for one second did Solange intend to let Eddi go.

THAT EVENING AFTER DINNER Eddi disappeared. She'd insisted she needed to be excused and she never returned. Doug had watched her go into one of the powder rooms on the first floor, but she had, evidently, slipped out when he looked away to respond to something Thurston said. The man had arrived earlier in the day and had stayed for dinner. He was none too happy that Solange still intended to introduce

Eddi to the board of directors on Wednesday despite his sudden reservations.

Thurston apparently had his own ideas about how this production should be handled. He was now in no hurry for Eddi to gain any power over the D'Martine fortune. Doug didn't like his pushiness where the matter was concerned. Solange liked it even less and told him so, at which time he promptly ended the discussion.

Excusing himself, Doug took the stairs two at a time and went in search of Eddi. Since the powder room she'd vacated was near the stairs, he assumed she had gone upstairs. Maybe to call her parents or maybe simply to be alone. Either way, he didn't want her out of his sight. Things were starting to get tense in the D'Martine household, mainly due to Thurston's stand on legal issues. He knew from the monitor built into his watch that she was still in the house. The tracking device he'd placed behind her ear sent a clear, steady signal.

When Doug found Eddi's bedroom door open he went on instant alert. He reached beneath his jacket and withdrew his weapon. The clink of metal against porcelain tugged him toward the room's en suite bathroom. He moved silently across the carpeted floor until he stood outside the partially open door. Straining to listen, he made out the sound of metal against metal echoing from the room. He gave the door a little push and it swung inward soundlessly. His gaze went immediately to the figure sitting astride the bathtub's outer ledge.

Eddi.

Exhaling some of his tension, he put his weapon away and rasped his knuckles against the door frame.

Startled by the unexpected intrusion, Eddi twisted around to look at him. She pressed her hand to her chest. "Doggone it, Doug, you scared the life out of me."

A frown formed between his eyes as he assessed the situation. She had dismantled the tub's elegant faucet. Parts were scattered across the closed toilet lid and on the floor near her foot. His gaze lingered on the ankle belonging to that foot then slid upward, along the shapely calf and over the knee to the partially exposed thigh. Her position astride the edge of the tub had forced the hem of her skirt high on her thighs, but she didn't seem to notice or care.

"Sorry," he offered, his gaze still distracted by the creamy, smooth thigh he had not seen before. "I was worried when you disappeared on me."

She blew out a heavy breath and turned her attention to the faucet. "I didn't want to hear any more from that lawyer. I don't like him. And I'm pretty sure he doesn't like me."

Doug moved into the room and propped a hip on the marble vanity counter. "Attorneys are cautious that way," he suggested, hoping to ease her distress, though he sensed the same feelings in the arrogant man himself.

"I still don't like him," she countered petulantly as she picked up a piece of expensive brass and shoved it back into place.

"Where did you get those tools?" He was relatively sure she hadn't packed any wrenches in her luggage. There hadn't been room.

"James rounded them up for me," she said, her attention focused on the task rather than on the conversation.

Doug smiled. Only Eddi, he mused.

"I couldn't stand that dripping," she explained. "Don't rich people know plumbers?"

Doug wasn't sure if she really expected an answer, but he gave her one anyway. "Since this is a guest room, it's likely that no one had noticed the problem."

"Well, her water bill should be a little less next month." And just like that the luxurious brass faucet was back together and not a leak in sight.

She pushed up from her position, drawing her leg over the tub's edge. "I'll have to get these back to James. He's been really nice to me." She gathered the tools and then smoothed a hand over her blouse as if suddenly aware that he was staring at her.

He hadn't meant to stare, but there was just something irresistible about a woman with a wrench in her hand. "I'll go with you."

Color tinged her cheeks only making her look more tempting. "Don't worry," she said, remorse weighing heavy in her tone. "I'm not going to beg you to kiss me again tonight."

Doug blocked her path when she would have walked past him. "For the record," he told her, knowing damn well he should leave it alone, "you wouldn't have to beg."

"EVERYTHING IS FALLING into place."

Joe listened to the voice on the other end of the line. They could have had this discussion in person, after all he was on the island now. But his partner was too cautious for that. He didn't want to take any chances on some witness coming out of the woodwork and putting two and two together after the fact.

Joe didn't like being ordered around, but he would do what he had to for now. A knowing grin slid across his lips. He'd have the last laugh anyway.

"I watched them on the cliffs today," his partner went on with wicked glee. "This unexpected turn is going to facilitate our plan. And this time we'll be rich."

Yes sir, Joe agreed silently, they would be rich all right, but only one of them would live to enjoy it.

Chapter Ten

Eddi appeared more comfortable at the D'Martine estate by Wednesday. Doug was relieved to see her relax a little. She'd spoken to her parents in Meadowbrook each morning and each evening, which helped tremendously to ease her anxiety. If Solange D'Martine resented Eddi's ever-present talk of her parents back home, Solange did a masterful job of concealing her displeasure.

Most of the previous day had been spent going over the history of the jewel trade and the D'Martines' various interests, international and domestic. Sort of a crash course in the family business. Eddi had no trouble catching on and seemed genuinely interested in the workings of the D'Martine empire. Solange was definitely pleased. Doug learned that it was Solange herself who had designed a great many of the classic pieces in their line. Since her son had possessed the same talent for creative designs, she hoped that trait had been passed on to his daughter. Eddi considered the chances dubious at best since she'd never designed anything that didn't include plumber's putty and pipes.

His gaze drifted to her, as was par for the course whenever she was in the same room. The navy slacks and jacket combined with her pleasant and attentive air gave her the appearance of elegance and sophistication matching that of anyone in the room. But he knew that beneath that polished exterior was a regular girl who didn't need riches to make her a lady.

There had been no more talk of kisses, despite his outright invitation. He could have throttled himself for not thinking before speaking. He'd intended to assuage her conscience for needing a distraction and using him; instead, he'd left an open invitation for more dangling in the air like a carrot on a stick.

Watching her now, seated next to her grandmother on a small sofa in the enormous parlor awaiting the arrival of the final board member, the urge to pursue this physical attraction between them was all but overpowering. But that would be against all the rules. Not to mention that he had not been completely honest with Eddi about who he was. No relationship should start out with any kind of deception hovering over it. Though his reasons for keeping his background secret were well intended, he wasn't sure Eddi would see it that way.

Doug glanced at his watch—5:20. The remaining guest who had not arrived was beyond fashionably late at this point. The other seven members, as well as the CEO, were already seated around the room, cocktails in hand, brusque business expressions in place. Doug sensed that one or more of those present weren't happy with what was about to go down.

He stayed on the fringes of the gathering, choosing to stand near a window, one shoulder propped against the ornate frame. Observations were best made from a slight distance, he had learned.

At 5:25, the butler, James Montgomery, showed the tardy board member into the room.

"I apologize for the delay," the man announced without preamble. "Traffic was stalled on the mainland, which required my taking a later ferry." He settled into the empty chair next to Thurston. "Shall we get started?"

The butler served the late arrival a drink and offered to refill those of the other guests. Doug didn't miss the way Montgomery smiled at Eddi as he passed her. The two of them had become good friends rather quickly, it seemed. Most of the staff liked her very much already. Doug surveyed the crowd of ruthless businessmen. In a few moments they would know how the other team felt about Eddi.

When the last introduction was out of the way, Thurston officially started the meeting.

"Ladies." He nodded to Solange and Eddi, then to the others present. "Gentlemen. This special meeting has been called to make you aware of certain changes prior to public announcement."

"I don't like this," CEO Kirk Wellfounder interjected abruptly. "I believe any sort of official announcement would only undermine our standing in the marketplace."

Solange sent him an assessing glare. "And how have you come to this conclusion, Kirk?" Her tone was calm and pleasant, but there was no ignoring the ferocity beneath.

Wellfounder stole a glance at Thurston. "Brandon, you and I have discussed this subject at length. With the American designers making a rebound of late, the last thing we need is any sign of weakness.''

Thurston looked a little startled that his disagreeable thoughts had been brought into the discussion. ''Well, now, Kirk, let's not be hasty—''

''How do you propose that the publicity surrounding my granddaughter could be negative?'' Solange stiffened her spine in defiance. ''I would think that the prospect of new blood would only strengthen our hold on the largest portion of the domestic as well as the international market.''

Eddi's discomfort level had just blasted to somewhere in the vicinity of the moon. This man, Mr. Wellfounder, didn't like her…didn't want her involved.

Maybe he was right….

Mr. Wellfounder looked a little nervous now. He glanced at Mr. Thurston again. ''You know the press will have a field day with what happened…to Edouard. Though clearly Miss Harper is a D'Martine,'' he offered, allowing his gaze to light on her ever so briefly, ''there will be speculation as to why she is being introduced at this time.''

''What are you implying?'' her grandmother D'Martine demanded.

After a heavy breath, Mr. Wellfounder said what was on his mind, ''At your age, some will perceive this move as an indication that you are no longer able to carry on the family tradition of D'Martine designs.''

Infinite silence fell over the room. Kind of the way it did when Eddi was waiting to see if a newly repaired joint would leak. Nobody moved or spoke, they simply sat there waiting for the next move, hoping the worst wouldn't happen. Eddi suddenly found herself wondering if the suits all these old guys were wearing were as pricey as they looked. A bubble of hysteria rose in her throat. Okay, she was losing ground here. Though she was pretty sure that the sum total of designer business wear in the room could feed a small country for a year, it wasn't really relevant at the moment.

Tension coiled so tightly inside her that she could scarcely breathe. Solange D'Martine was getting on up there, that was true, but it didn't mean she was out of the game. But Eddi didn't miss Wellfounder's point. In business, even in a small-town hardware store and plumbing service, public perception was everything.

"Maybe," she said, shocked that she'd actually spoken out loud. All gazes shifted to her. Well, she'd started it now, she might as well finish. "Maybe this isn't a good idea." She turned to her grandmother. "I don't want to cause any trouble. If my involvement is going to—"

"Miss Harper," an elderly gentleman, a Mr. Pogue if she remembered correctly, interrupted, "our only concern is for your safety. If there is any risk involved in making your presence public, then perhaps we should rethink our strategy."

"That's why we have Mr. Cooper," Solange reminded firmly. The room's attention swung to Doug. "He will ensure that no harm comes to my granddaughter until the media frenzy passes. Further need for personal security will be assessed at that time."

At that time? Eddi had to get back home soon. She

wasn't about to let that knucklehead Lamar steal all her business.

"Are you really prepared for the past to be publicly resurrected as you know it will be?" the CEO wanted to know. "They will rehash every painful detail. If the perpetrators of Edouard's murder are still out there, isn't this like waving a red flag?"

Doug straightened from his relaxed stance and took a few steps in the direction of the group, again garnering everyone's regard. Eddi couldn't help a smile. She felt safe as long as he was nearby. And there was that zing of electricity that zipped through her each time she looked at him. He looked right at home with this highbrow crowd. Doug had evidently done his research and she was so thankful for his presence. Victoria Colby had definitely picked the right man for the job.

"Mr. Wellfounder," Doug said, addressing the CEO, "there is no compelling reason to believe that the perpetrators of a twenty-five-year-old crime—if they are even still alive—would pursue a second attempt. As Miss Harper's personal security, my primary concern is that a copycat might attempt to pull off something similar. You have my full assurance that as long as Miss Harper is with me, she will be safe from harm."

Pride and admiration welled inside Eddi. Now, *there* was a hero. The kind she read about in romance novels. The same ones depicted in old black-and-white movies when men were men and women—she chewed her lower lip as she considered the truth of the matter—weren't plumbers.

"But the media frenzy—"

"Will pass," Solange cut off the rest of Mr. Wellfounder's protest. "This, gentlemen," she said with a sweep of her hand in Eddi's direction, "is my granddaughter. Heir to the very corporation that employs each and every one of you. She will be treated with the same respect and courtesy that you have shown me during the past quarter century. Are there any other questions?"

Eddi was greatly relieved when all eight members of the board of directors, as well as the CEO, stood, and one at a time offered his hand in agreement of the matter. She supposed actions spoke louder than words since no one bothered to answer her grandmother's question, but all, including the lawyer Thurston, made a grand show of welcoming her aboard. Eddi wasn't so sure she wanted to be aboard, but her grandmother had convinced her that it was necessary. This step would not prevent her from returning to her life back home. She would attend the quarterly business meetings and sit in on biannual meetings with the designers. That Eddi could handle. A quick trip to New York twice a year and regular visits to the D'Martine estate were no big deal. She fully intended to visit her newly discovered grandmother every chance she got.

Honestly, she hadn't expected it to be this simple. Now, once the social courtesies were out of the way, there would be a mound of paperwork for her to sign. Her grandmother had warned her that it would be extensive. Mr. Thurston had been preparing documents for days.

When the guests were gone, they relocated to the library. James, the only butler she'd ever known and her new friend, had served tea. Seated at the magnificent desk that had belonged to her grandfather with Doug on one side and her grandmother on the other, Eddi signed document after document. Mr. Thurston briefly explained each. By the time they reached the final one, her hand had started to cramp.

"This one you will want to pay particular attention to, Miss Harper," Thurston said with something like condescension in his tone.

The document pertained to a trust fund that provided a staggering annual sum for Eddi's use. "What's this?" She looked from the document to her grandmother. "This is too much money." She shook her head. "I can't accept this."

Solange met her confusion with granitelike determination. "This money is yours. This and a great deal more. You will use it as you see fit."

Eddi sighed wearily. This was simply too much. "I want to help my folks back home," she confessed. "But this—" she stared at the figures once more "—this is a great deal more than what I need."

"Please, Miss Harper," Thurston urged with a roll of his eyes, "dispense with the theatrics and sign it."

"Brandon," Solange said sharply, "you have been my most trusted confidant for thirty years. I don't want that to change, but your own *theatrics* today have given me pause."

Eddi quickly signed the paper. "Here you go." She passed it to the lawyer in hopes of drenching the fury that sounded ready to ignite in her grandmother's tone. She didn't want to be the cause of division or trouble of any sort.

"All right." Thurston arranged the papers into a

neat stack and transferred them to his briefcase. "I'll file these as appropriate." He beamed a smile at Solange that looked more than a little strained. "I'll see all of you tomorrow evening at the gala."

Solange held him in place with a mere look for several tension-filled beats before saying, "We're not finished with this matter, Brandon. I will know the reason you chose to speak with the members of the board behind my back. Another time," she added with a dismissive nod.

Mr. Thurston appeared a bit peaked when he left the study. Something else for Eddi to feel guilty about. The man was only trying to protect Solange's best interests. Even though Eddi didn't like him much, that's what attorneys did, right?

"I don't want to cause trouble," Eddi said again, hoping to get the point across this time. "These people have been loyal to you all these years. They're just worried that some stranger has shown up to throw a wrench in the works."

Solange patted Eddi's hand. "Don't concern yourself with that nonsense, my dear. We all have our place in this life and lucky for me I'm the boss." She smiled. "As you will be someday."

Pushing numbly to her feet, Eddi stood next to Doug as her grandmother rose and left the room. For a woman of seventy-two, Solange D'Martine moved with a grace that was mastered by few. But did she really know what she was doing giving Eddi all this control? What did Eddi know about the jewelry industry? Nothing, except what little she'd absorbed during the past two days. *She knew nothing.* The board and CEO were right to be concerned. What if her grandmother suddenly died? How in the world would Eddi handle all this new responsibility?

"What have I done?"

The words were scarcely a whisper but Doug understood completely. He moved in closer and placed a reassuring hand on her arm. "You've done the right thing," he consoled. "The only thing you could."

Eddi shook her head, tears welling in her eyes, fear pumping through her veins. All of this suddenly felt wrong somehow. But she was committed. Had just signed her name to the whole kit and caboodle.

"I have to get out of here," she murmured and swiped at a rebel tear that escaped her savage hold on her emotions. "I need to think. I can't think here."

Doug gifted her with one of those smiles that made her shiver all the way to her toes. "I know just the place to go."

THE MUSIC THUMPED loudly, vibrating the very walls of the eclectic nightclub. Bodies gyrated on the dance floor to the fast, contemporary beat. Others, dressed in all styles of avant-garde apparel, clung to the long, sleek bar that curved its way around one side of the popular night spot. The Atlantic Connection had not changed in the least during Doug's five-year hiatus from the social scene on the island.

The music was still loud, the patrons still enthusiastic and the ambience still conducive to intimacy and invisibility. The already dim lighting was further muted by the haze of smoke hugging the ceiling.

Eddi had discarded the sophisticated jacket, boldly choosing to wear only the coordinating silk camisole in the same navy as her well-fitting slacks. Doug would have forgone his own jacket were it not for the nine-millimeter he wore in the shoulder holster. An armed man was anything but inconspicuous.

He skipped the tables around the dance floor, deciding they lacked the privacy he needed for more than one reason. The bar was out of the question, just in case anyone he used to know still worked here. What they needed was a dark, tucked-away corner. After spotting the one unoccupied booth in the place, he ushered Eddi toward it. Close enough. Once seated he leaned down and asked, "What would you like to drink?"

She shrugged. "I don't know. Wine? What would you suggest?"

He thought about that for a moment. It hadn't occurred to him that she might be a virgin in more than one respect. He'd have to tread carefully here, getting a principal drunk was definitely not in his job description. However, this was her last night as a private citizen, in a manner of speaking, and he wanted to make it memorable. He wanted her to forget everything for just this one night. In truth, he would like a great deal more than that, but he would not overstep his bounds. He'd already made that mistake once. He refused to allow it to happen again.

"How about a cosmopolitan?" he suggested. It was more or less a ladies' drink and quite agreeable with the palate even if one wasn't accustomed to alcohol.

"Sounds okay to me." The stress of the last few days lessened visibly as she took in the decadent, sexy atmosphere in one long sweep of her gaze. "I've never been to a nightclub before."

He'd thought as much. "Do you dance?"

Color bloomed on her cheeks. "I don't think so."

Two cosmopolitans later and Eddi was ready for her first foray onto the floor. Despite the buzz the last drink had induced, she was still a little nervous. She didn't have to say anything; Doug could read the hesitation in her eyes.

He pulled her into his arms and smiled. "We could always slow dance," he offered.

She glanced around at the shimmying torsos. "I don't think slow dancing really goes with this music."

He tucked her arms around his neck, settled his on her hips and drew her nearer. "Then we'll set a new trend."

She giggled nervously, but didn't resist. "Okay."

Ignoring the loud music vibrating from the speakers, Doug set the rhythm, moving painstakingly slowly to a beat that came from within. She mimicked his every move with a naiveté and wonder that made his protective instincts surge more strongly than ever before.

The tempo eventually slowed as one song faded into another, this one a romantic tune that was all the rage on the airwaves and video scene. His own slow movements blended with the sensual beat, drawing out the languid motions until his body hardened with a tension that had nothing to do with the music and everything to do with the woman in his arms.

She looked up at him, her eyes liquid with heat and a need she couldn't possibly fully understand. "Am I doing okay?" she asked tentatively.

He nodded, his gaze drawn to those lush lips. His

mind instantly summoning the memory of her taste. She smiled and his heart skipped a beat.

"Thank you," she murmured.

He inclined his head to the right and studied her a second or two. "For what?" Having the foresight to choose a rental car versus being picked up by the D'Martine chauffeur when they arrived thus making this little escape possible? he wondered.

She shrugged lightly. "Oh, I don't know. For being you? For not only keeping me safe but for keeping me straight—" Her eyes sparkled mischievously. "Discounting tonight, of course. You can't imagine how important being able to trust you has been during this whole…ordeal."

Guilt tapped at his conscience, but he exiled it. "I won't let you down, Eddi. Whatever happens, you can count on me."

She moistened her lips and then suddenly stopped moving. Doug stopped as well and waited for her to say whatever was on her mind.

"Remember when you said that I didn't have to beg?"

He nodded, the move wooden with ambivalence. He'd only had one beer, but between her sweet body in his arms and the seductive environment, it wouldn't take much more to push him over the edge.

"I'd like you to kiss me again."

And just like that—he fell.

Chapter Eleven

"Maybe we should call it a night," Doug suggested. A new kind of tension tightened inside him. Coming here had been an error in judgment. He'd wanted to take her away from all the stress and expectation of what was to come. Between the meeting with the board of directors and the signing session with Thurston, Eddi had been through too much and needed a break.

Damn, but that all sounded so gallant of him. But he'd been anything but gallant. He'd brought her to a place where he could ply her with drink and hold her in his arms. Because he was a selfish, thoughtless cad who lusted after her when she was her most vulnerable. Like right now.

Hurt and confusion clouded her expression. "But I don't want to go back. I want to..." She looked deeply into his eyes, her own filled with yearning. "I want to be with you."

With every fiber of his being he'd wanted to hear those words on a level that he only just recognized. He confessed now that he'd wanted her almost from the moment he saw her standing in the doorway of her mother's living room. The overalls hadn't put him off in the least. He'd been intrigued, only to later become captivated and then infatuated.

But that's all this could be. He wouldn't give himself credit for anything more, like true love. And anything less was simply unacceptable. Eddi deserved a great deal more.

"Come with me." He took her by the hand and led her through the crowd still moving to the music. They needed privacy for this discussion, but not the kind of privacy that would allow the moment to escalate further out of control.

"Doug! Whoa! Man, is that you?"

A blast from the past slammed into Doug's gut, drawing him to a startled halt.

"It is you!" A hand whopped him on the back. "Long time no see."

Doug looked to his right and straight into the eyes of one of his old college roommates. A guy he'd partied with summer after summer in this very club. The magnitude of the mistake he'd made in coming here tonight struck him all over again with the impact of a physical blow. His hand tightened on Eddi's. He didn't want her to find out this way. Until now, who or what he'd been in the past hadn't really been relevant, but suddenly it mattered a great deal.

"Hey, Carl." Doug shook his old pal's hand. "It has been a long time."

Carl sized him up, then leaned slightly to the left to get a look at Eddi. "Edwinna, this is an old friend of mine, Carl Spokes," Doug relented when Carl forced the issue by extending his hand in her direction.

"Nice to meet you, Carl." Eddi smiled politely.

"Likewise," Carl said with a lecherous leer.

Doug's jaw clenched. He would not let things go down this way. Considering the guy's escapades, Doug could just imagine what his old friend was thinking at the moment.

He leaned toward him. "Can we play catch-up later? I really have to go right now." He gave Carl a knowing look. "If you know what I mean."

"Yeah." Carl glanced at Eddi. "Sure, man." He stabbed an accusing finger at Doug. "But don't shove off without dropping by to see me, buddy. I want to know where the hell you've been. You can't just drop off the face of the planet like that—"

Doug gave him a two-fingered salute. "I'll catch up with you in a day or two." He dived into the crowd, dragging Eddi with him before Carl could say anything else. Well, plan A was out. Doug had considered taking Eddi to the smaller, quieter bar next door, but that was out of the question now. He couldn't risk running into anyone else from his past.

He'd been an idiot once tonight. He wasn't about to make the same mistake twice. He hadn't expected to run into any of his old summer pals this late in the year, but that had been a serious lapse in judgment.

"I didn't know you had friends here," Eddi said as he ushered her into the car.

"Carl and I attended college together," he told her without telling her anything at all and hopefully avoided answering the question altogether.

Doug backed out of the parking slot and pulled onto the street and decided that going back to the D'Martine residence was the proper thing to do.

"I don't want to go back yet," she said, clearly reading his mind. God, he hoped not.

He considered the possible options. There was a coffee shop on Circuit Avenue. He glanced at the digital clock on the dash. Too early for the party crowd to start filtering in. That would likely be the least troublesome alternative.

"There's a place I know where we can talk."

She sighed. He read the disappointment and hurt in the sound. "I guess that's better than nothing."

If she only knew how much more he wanted than merely to talk. His hesitation in acting on that desire was about more than his tardy sense of professionalism kicking in; he knew she was confused right now. She needed reassurances, and the attraction between them had been building to the breaking point. Giving in to the mutual need felt like the right thing to do. But he knew better. He was older and far more experienced than Eddi. He knew that sex was not the answer she sought.

Conversely, he was a man. Sex seemed like a perfect answer to him, but that was a physical, knee-jerk response. He had to consider the consequences and there would be plenty. Not only would he be failing where his assigned duties were concerned, he would be failing as a human being. Taking advantage of Eddi that way would be wrong. As confusing as his own feelings for her were concerned, he couldn't muddy the waters any further. She drew him on more levels than anyone else ever had, but it could simply be his empathy for her circumstances or the intense sweetness she personified. There were far too many

variables to make a sound call. For that reason, he
had to prevent either of them from crossing that line.

Eddi would thank him for it later.

Even if she didn't realize it now.

The coffee shop Doug selected as their next des-
tination looked pretty much deserted at this hour of
the evening. Eddi imagined that most of those at the
local clubs would show up here after midnight since
the place stayed open all night long. Back in Meadowbrook they didn't have any places that stayed
open twenty-four hours a day. But then, they didn't
have any nightclubs either. It was only a short drive
from the cluster of nightspots they'd left behind, making this the logical place for relaxing after partying
down. Inside, the aroma of coffee smelled heavenly.
The variety of pastries displayed on white stoneware
behind meticulously clean glass looked scrumptious.

"Would you like coffee? A pastry?"

Eddi thought about that a moment and instantly a
plan came to her. "Decaf and one of those creamy-
looking things there." She pointed to the sticky,
sweet roll, then smiled innocently. "I'll get a table."

He nodded, looking more than a little confused at
her about-face. Well, he'd better get ready, she was
only slowing down to gather her scattered courage.

Eddi surveyed the small café and selected the intimate horseshoe-shaped booth in the very back of the
seating area. There was a little more light than she
would have preferred, but otherwise, the setting was
perfect. Classic big-band music emanated softly from
the overhead speakers. Old-fashioned bar stools with
red vinyl seats lined the bar. Checkered tablecloths
dressed the intimate tables for two and four. But the

few booths were by far the most romantic. The curved shape itself invited closeness. And there was plenty of privacy since there wasn't a soul on that side of the room.

Eddi scooted onto the worn soft seat and waited for Doug to find her. The look of surprise that claimed his handsome face when he noted that she had settled at the very back corner of the room made her smile. Just because he had all the experience and she had none didn't mean he was going to win the game. She'd read enough romance novels and seen enough movies to know how to set up a seduction. Plus, she hadn't been Most Valuable Player three years running back in high school for nothing.

Granted, she would need help—a lot of it—for the follow-through with this particular strategy, but she could definitely get the ball rolling.

When he'd settled in the booth she scooted around next to him, hip to hip, and then took a bite of the delicious pastry, putting on a show as she did. She licked her fingers, accompanying the deliberately slow, thorough act with satisfied sounds.

He watched. Swallowed hard, the play of tanned muscle along his throat momentarily distracting her. "Good?" The one word sounded strained, almost choked.

"Oh, yes." She reached for another bite. "Incredible." Her tongue darted out to swipe a bit of filling from her lower lip and she moaned.

Doug looked away, his hands wrapped around the stoneware mug as if it were a buoy in violent waters. So, he wasn't so unaffected. Good. He'd almost hurt her feelings when he'd suggested they call it a night.

Now, to go in for the kill.

Divide and conquer. She had to distract his mind while she tortured his body.

She'd seen it done in the movies. She just hoped it worked or she was going to end up looking more foolish than she feared she already did. As hard as he tried to pretend he wasn't interested, she knew he was. He was definitely attracted to her and that in itself was enough to shore up her shaky determination. She couldn't remember the last time a guy had looked at her the way Doug did. She hadn't been kissed in God knows how long and she'd *never* been kissed like that.

"Where did you and Carl go to college?"

Doug threw up his guard at the question. The change was subtle, but she saw it. The slightest stiffening of his shoulders. He didn't like talking about his past or his family. She wondered about that.

"Harvard," he admitted grudgingly.

Her eyes widened before she could stop the automatic reaction. "That...that's amazing." Harvard? She took another bite of the pastry just to occupy her mouth for fear she'd say something lame. She'd known Doug was smart and very polished. *But Harvard?*

"I probably should call and let someone know when we'll be back," he suggested in a blatant attempt to change the subject.

"Where does your family live?" she asked, ignoring his comment. She had the strangest feeling that she was about to uncover some family skeleton that he fiercely did not want her to know about. He shouldn't feel that way. He definitely knew her family's deepest, darkest one.

"Boston." His tone was clipped now. He did not want to tarry on this subject.

Too bad. Renewed enthusiasm struck Eddi. This was exactly the topic she needed to throw him off balance.

"You have brothers and sisters?" She snuggled her shoulder closer to his. "Older? Younger?"

"An older sister and a younger brother." He sipped his coffee, carefully keeping his gaze forward.

She dragged the tip of her forefinger through the pastry icing and then sucked it off. "What do your folks do for a living?" She made another of those appreciative sounds as she dipped for more icing.

"My father is—"

She pressed her fingertip to his lips. "Try it. You'll like it."

He stalled. She leaned nearer. "I swear it's heavenly," she murmured close to his ear before drawing away and prodding, "What were you saying about your father?"

Just as she'd known, instead of answering her question he licked her finger. Heat seared through her and she shivered. The feel of his hot tongue on her flesh made her want to weep for more. The memory of how that tongue had teased her lips when they'd kissed made her feminine muscles clench with anticipation. The intensity of the feeling was alien and at the same time utterly delightful. She wanted more.

"Tasty, isn't it?" she asked in the most seductive whisper she could manage.

He turned toward her then, his gaze going straight

to her mouth as if he'd tasted the words she'd spoken rather than the icing she'd offered.

"Yes."

She lifted her chin, putting her mouth nearer to his. Her heart thundered with equal measures anticipation and trepidation, but she couldn't stop now. "Let me see how it tastes on you."

He obeyed her command, moving closer until their lips just did touch. She licked those full, firm lips and made a tiny sound of satisfaction. He kissed her then, closing his mouth fully over hers, thrusting that wicked tongue deep inside. Her fingers threaded into that thick silky hair and urged him on. He didn't disappoint her. The pressure of his mouth on hers became more insistent, more demanding in its own right. She melted into him, reveling in the feel of his hard body as he twisted to meet her, chest to breasts.

As his possessive kiss went on and on, she allowed the fingers of one hand to slip downward, to learn the chiseled outline of his face. The smooth, broad forehead and square, slightly stubbled jaw, and downward to his corded neck and onto the sculpted terrain of his chest. She traced the ridges of muscle beneath the thin fabric of his shirt. Could feel the pounding of his heart. Her body burned to know him flesh to flesh. To touch him beneath the barrier of silk and summerweight wool he wore. Never in her entire life had she felt so alive...so incredibly needy. Though she couldn't name the want...she wanted oh so desperately.

His hungry mouth left hers and she whimpered, but a moan of encouragement escaped her when those skilled lips began a path along the length of her throat. He took his time, tasting and teasing. He didn't stop when he reached the silk of her camisole or the rise of her breasts. He kept on kissing her through the sensual fabric, adding to her pleasure until his mouth closed over her nipple and sucked. Her breath vacated her lungs, leaving her in a state so near to dying of pleasure she felt sure death must be imminent.

Her mind cleared of all thought, her focus narrowed until her world consisted only of him and the kaleidoscope of sensations he ignited inside her. Her body was a frenzy of heat and need. She wanted him to take her someplace more private and show her what this all meant…where it should go.

Plunging her fingers into his hair once more to urge him on, she arched her back, instinctively begging for more of his attention. His arms went around her waist. Her thigh came up to meet his hand as he cupped the swell of her bottom. Her knee hit the table. Stoneware rattled.

He stopped. Drew away from the breast he'd been suckling. His warm breath sent shivers over the engorged flesh beneath the dampened silk. His gaze lifted to hers and he blinked twice, shattering the haze that had shrouded them.

"I'm sorry." He straightened, turning away from her as he thrust a hand through his tousled hair.

Just like that, it was over. Her body vibrated with an ache that was at once instinctive yet unfamiliar. She'd been on the verge of something big, she realized. And he'd denied her that.

Darn it.

Tomorrow was a whole new and scary beginning for her. She'd decided tonight that she didn't want to wake up a virgin tomorrow. Maybe she was doomed to spend the rest of her now utterly confusing life alone, but she didn't have to spend it a virgin. That part of the curse she could do something about.

"You never did finish telling me what your father did for a living," she grumped. If she wasn't going to get sex out of this, at least she could have some answers about her mysterious bodyguard.

Doug sat up straighter and cleared his throat. "He's in banking." He allowed a brief glance in her direction. "We really should be getting back." He eased out of the booth looking more uneasy than she'd ever seen him.

Maybe she'd been fooling herself. Maybe he didn't want her quite the way she wanted him. One glance at the front of his trousers settled that issue. He was definitely aroused. That much was abundantly clear. Her tummy quivered.

"What about your mother?" she fished, trying not to sound annoyed as she slid out of the booth. He wasn't going to get away scot-free.

Doug tossed a tip on the table. "She's—" he thought about it a moment "—an art buff."

"She's like a collector?" Eddi wondered how he could sound so calm so quickly. Her whole body still strummed with the heat and shivery sensations he'd set alight inside her. She'd seen the proof of his need. How did he manage to appear so unaffected? She resisted the urge to shake herself. She had to focus here. Had to admit that he wasn't going to follow through with whatever he felt. Despite her best efforts she sighed as he led her from the cozy coffee shop. It had to be the curse.

The Club was right. She was doomed.

At the car Doug hesitated before opening her door. "Eddi, I apologize for my behavior. There's no excuse for my lack of professionalism."

Definitely the curse. The man was apologizing for kissing her for goodness' sake. How pathetic was that? Whoever heard of a guy doing that? The last of the fire he'd kindled died an instant death.

"It's okay," she told him. No use in ruining the evening for both of them. She might as well face facts. Though she had certainly garnered a reaction in him physically, who wanted a plumber for a girlfriend? Men like Doug preferred the classy, sophisticated type. Something she would never be, trust fund or not. Eddi was just plain old Eddi. "I understand." Might as well let him completely off the hook. "It's always been this way. Guys just aren't interested in a relationship with women like me."

Doug drove back to the D'Martine estate in silence. He wanted to correct Eddi on her assumption. The idea that guys had looked at her as anything other than a beautiful woman infuriated him. When he looked at her he saw a sweet, vulnerable young lady who was not only beautiful, but talented as well. If some other guy saw less then he was the one lacking, not Eddi.

But telling her so would be a mistake. It had taken every ounce of willpower he possessed to pull out of that intimate embrace back there in the coffee shop. He wanted her in a way that, frankly, scared him. Not only would it be the wrong thing to do on a professional level, but taking advantage of her attraction to him would simply be wrong on a personal level. He hadn't been completely honest with her. Falling into a relationship without knowing all the facts was bad enough when a person had the appropriate experience to make an informed decision. Eddi was completely inexperienced. She had nothing on which to compare how she felt.

No matter how badly he wanted to, he would protect her from herself…as well as him. He sincerely doubted his chivalry could withstand another onslaught of her attempts at seducing him. He was certain she was merely confused, desperate for a distraction…any kind of relief from present circumstances. He was simply handy. The foolish thing was that reality did little to lessen his own desire to allow her to do just as she pleased. At this point he was barely hanging on to his honor.

The house was quiet when they entered at nearly midnight. All Doug had to do was check out her room, say good-night and close the door. He could struggle with the physical consequences of walking away with a long, cold shower. It was the right thing, he told himself again.

Eddi stood by while he performed the usual checks of her personal security. The longer she watched him move the more determined she was that she had to have this one night. Just this one. If she was cursed, doomed to be an old maid the rest of her life, at least she'd have one night to remember. If he was too much of a gentleman to "take advantage" of her, as he had insinuated, well then, she'd just have to take advantage of him. She shivered at the prospect.

While hc finished his survey, she kicked off her shoes and leaned against the closed door. With a smile she reached behind her and locked it. Everyone in the house was asleep; no one would ever know.

"Everything is as it should be," he announced with a smile that seemed a little weary. He looked just a tad rumpled from their making out in the close confines of the booth. But mainly he looked as handsome as sin and as sexy as all get out.

"Mr. Cooper," she began in the most authoritative tone she could muster, one very similar to the one she'd heard her grandmother use with that smart-aleck lawyer. "Do you or do you not work for me?"

A vague frown of confusion stole across his forehead. "In a manner of speaking. I was actually hired by Mrs. D'Martine, but…" His frown deepened. "What's going on, Eddi?" he asked, clearly suspicious now.

She folded her arms over her chest and leveled a gaze on him that she felt certain was nothing short of unyielding. "Well, since you work for me, you are required to obey my wishes."

His gaze narrowed. "What is it that you wish?"

A smile slid across her lips. "Take off your clothes, Mr. Cooper."

There was a stillness about him that told her he was weighing his options carefully before proceeding. "Now, please," she insisted.

"Isn't that sexual harassment?" he asked cautiously.

She shrugged. "Depends on how you look at it I suppose."

"Eddi." He came closer, her pulse reacted instantly. "I know what you're doing, but I promise you it would be a mistake. One I'm certain you don't want to make.''

"Ah, but you're wrong," she countered. "I've spent my whole life being a good little girl." She pushed off from the door and closed the distance between them. "Just for tonight, I want to be bad. Do you have a problem with that, Mr. Cooper?''

He was breathing harder now, she could see the rapid rise and fall of his chest. The firm set of his lips softened making her heart thump harder.

One long pulse-pounding moment passed before he responded. "Miss Harper, I do believe you've had too much excitement. Perhaps you should sleep on this proposal and we can discuss it tomorrow.''

She shook her head resolutely from side to side. "No more waiting. Now, take off your clothes.''

Something like a challenge flashed in his eyes. "You're certain about this?''

"Absolutely.''

He was going to do it! The challenge in those blue eyes morphed into determination. Eddi's breath caught and held in her throat, right behind the knot of tension lodged there.

The elegant jacket hit the floor first. Then the leather shoulder holster and the big, mean-looking gun dropped down next to it. Her eyes widened with anticipation as he slowly released button after button, drawing out the wait. When he finally shrugged out of the shirt, she gasped. Wide, wide shoulders narrowed into a lean waist, and the terrain in between was simply awesome. Ridges and planes of sculpted muscle and just a sprinkling of dark hair. She'd seen her share of guys in swim trunks at the lake, but never had she seen anyone like Doug in real life. On television maybe or in some magazine. But never, ever had she laid eyes on anything like this in the flesh.

Her heart hammered so hard she could hardly breathe. He watched her every reaction, read her like an open book as he toed off his shoes. She knew this because she saw it in his eyes…in the ghost of a smile that lingered on those sexy lips.

Leather hissed as he dragged his belt free of his trousers. Then he reached for the fly and the sound of the zipper sliding downward echoed in the silence of the room. Her mouth went completely dry.

The trousers dropped to his ankles and he kicked them aside. Long, muscular legs and silk paisley boxers completed the picture.

"What now, Miss Harper?" he asked, his voice husky.

Her gaze locked on a scar on his left side, small but jagged. "What…" She moistened her lips. "What happened?" She didn't have to clarify.

"Hazard of the job."

She blinked, only now realizing that his job could be dangerous. That thought only made her more desperate to touch him.

She swallowed tightly and firmed her waning courage. "The rest," she mumbled, unable to say the exact words.

He cocked his head toward his shoulder. She stood so close to him now she could see the tension radiating through every honed muscle of his body.

"I'm not doing this alone, my lady," he murmured. "Before I go any further, you're going to have to show me just how *bad* you intend to be."

Then she understood. He thought he'd scare her off. If *she* had to play, too, she'd lose her nerve.

Well, he just didn't get it. She was one determined, however doomed, woman.

"Fine." She turned back to the door just long enough to flip off the overhead light, leaving them in near darkness save for the one table lamp in the sitting area on the far side of the room.

While he observed her intently, she slowly, mimicking the moves she'd learned from him moments before, undressed. When she stood there in nothing but the camisole and her panties, she stopped. Resisting the urge to shield herself with her arms, she squared her shoulders, leveled her gaze on his, hard as that proved, and forced a smile. "It's your move."

Chapter Twelve

It was at that moment that Doug fully comprehended just how serious Eddi was about this.

She intended to have sex with him whatever the consequences.

For the first time in his life he wished for the inability to properly respond. It was insane, he knew, but the lack of physical ability was the only possible solution to his current dilemma. There was no way in hell he could stand here and not react to her, emotionally as well as physically. And that made the matter all the worse. It wasn't just his physical reaction that posed difficulties, it went far deeper than that. He wanted to please her...wanted to know her. That simply couldn't happen, not while he was on the job.

Fine time to consider that, he mused as he stood before her naked save for his shorts. He'd let her goad him into this and now they stood here, staring at each other with hunger in their eyes and each waiting on the other to make the next move.

He was in serious trouble here.

With clear purpose she closed the remaining distance between them, but he didn't miss the fine shiver that swept over her as she paused directly in front of him.

"Show me what all the fuss is about," she ordered softly. "You've taught me how to dress, how to walk, how to react amid the socially elite. Teach me this."

He was dead.

No way in hell could he turn her down....

Just looking into those devastatingly innocent blue eyes sapped the final remnants of his resolve.

He started to reach for her but hesitated. *Innocent* was the key word here. Though she was almost twenty-five, she'd spent her entire adult life struggling to keep her family afloat financially and to hang on to the family business. From all accounts, she'd forgone any kind of social life. She deserved for her first time to be special. Doug didn't doubt that he could make it very special for her, but would it be fair to her? Yes, they were attracted to each other. More than that even. But she'd waited all this time, she should share this moment with the man with whom she planned to spend the rest of her life.

That probably wasn't going to be him. An ache settled heavily upon his chest. He didn't understand it, didn't even try. Instead, he decided to focus on making Eddi feel like the beautiful young woman she was without taking away the treasured moment that only her future husband deserved the right to take.

Maybe he was more gallant than he'd given himself credit. An inner voice railed at that suggestion. Okay, more likely he was simply scared to death of where making love with her would lead. She was an assignment...his job...he had to remember that.

But he could give her a taste of what she'd been

missing. Give her the distraction she longed for. He could be her first in one way.

"I know you want to," she murmured, that expectant gaze searching his.

He touched her cheek with his fingertips, watched the flare of desire in her eyes. Felt that same heat flow through his veins. "I can't deny that." He leaned down and kissed that soft cheek. "You may be the boss, but we're going to do this my way."

Before she could argue, his mouth claimed hers. He kissed her until they were both breathless, then he led her to the bed. After ushering her down onto the edge, he knelt in front of her. Need and desire pumping through him, he removed the camisole. His breath caught at the modest beauty of her small, firm breasts. Slowly, thoroughly, he laved her sweet flesh with his mouth. He kissed, licked and suckled until she trembled and cried out his name. Then, using one hand splayed over her chest, he pressed her down onto the bed. Scarcely breathing in an attempt to slow the want clamoring for his attention, he dragged the silky panties down her long, toned legs and then off those delicate ankles. He spread her thighs and kissed her intimately. Her fingers fisted in the elegant bed linens as her body arched like a bow. His heart raced with the need he continued to deny and he plunged toward release though only his mouth and hands touched her sweet body. But that was all it took. The feel of her porcelain-smooth skin…the smell and taste of her dewy softness.

Shaking with the intensity of his own desire, he took his time, tasting, touching, teasing until she slipped over the edge, falling headlong into her first-ever sexual release. And it was her first. The surprise and awe was in every sound she uttered, every move she made as she went rigid, then boneless with satiation.

She reached for him. Took his face in her hands and pulled his mouth to hers. She kissed him, surprised all over again and then reveling in the taste of her own sensuality. He hovered just above her, every muscle taut with the effort of keeping his body an inch or so apart from hers. Suddenly her legs encircled his waist and she drew him intimately against her. Her feminine heat seared through his silk boxers. He groaned with the pleasure of it. She echoed the same.

To his startled amazement he did something he hadn't done since junior high—he came in his shorts.

EDDI STOOD BEFORE THE full-length mirror in her room. She had to admit, she looked pretty darn good in the dress Doug had helped her select for tonight's gala event. The royal blue went well with her coloring and the sheath fit like a glove. The material was sleek and smooth, not too flashy, but not too demure either. The matching heels were the lower ones she preferred.

The diamond studs that dazzled from her earlobes were especially precious to her. Her grandmother Solange had said that she'd received them as a gift as a young girl from her father and insisted that Eddi have them now. The elegant but understated corsage she wore on her wrist was from Doug. She'd made the mistake of mentioning that she'd never been to anything like this. The closest thing had been her high-school prom and she hadn't gotten anything from her date except a wrestling match when he'd copped a feel. Being the terrific guy he was, Doug had gone all out to make this night special, including the corsage.

But nothing about tonight would compare to last night. She looked at herself again. Though technically she was still a virgin, she felt different now. She felt more like a woman. Doug had definitely awakened the woman in her and she hungered desperately for the opportunity to return the favor, in a manner of speaking. If the preview was any indication of how mind-blowing the main event was, she couldn't wait to take the next step.

Her heart skipped a beat or two each time she thought of him. She knew she had fallen head over heels for the guy and he'd tried a dozen ways to slow her descent. That just made her love him all the more. But last night, when he'd selflessly brought her the single most pleasurable moment in her life, she had known that men like Douglas Cooper only came along once in a lifetime. He was a true gentleman, a trusted friend, and would be a skilled lover. He'd certainly made her a happy woman with just his hands and that awesome mouth.

She moistened her lips and decided, whether he was willing or not, she intended to give tit for tat the first chance she got. Like maybe tonight after the party was over. She shivered at the prospect.

A light rap on the door jerked her from her lust-arousing scheming. With one last check of the French twist she'd managed to wrangle her hair into, she hurried to the door.

Something in her chest shifted the moment her gaze collided with Doug's.

He smiled and she melted completely. "You look wonderful."

She managed a nod. "You don't look so bad yourself." Actually, he looked incredible as usual. The cut of the tailored suit was enough to make her salivate. But the truly sexy part was that he was so at ease with himself. If the man possessed one arrogant bone, she hadn't found it.

"Why, thank you, Miss Harper." His gaze swept over her again. "Shall we?" He offered his arm.

As she curled her arm around his, Eddi considered that she'd thought long and hard about Douglas Cooper and had decided that he was a self-made man. He'd worked hard to accomplish what he had achieved. He was like her...sort of. A small part of her couldn't help hoping that somehow they could pursue this attraction that sizzled between them. But he'd go back to Chicago as soon as her grandmother deemed there was no threat to the newly found D'Martine heir. Just another reason Eddi had to find some way to make herself memorable to the guy. Even after he'd gone back home to Chicago, she wanted him to think about her day and night...until he just had to come back.

Midway down the staircase, she paused and took a moment to admire the enormous painting of the D'Martine family. She wondered if she would ever know the kind of love and commitment her grandmother and grandfather had known. The same kind her mom and dad had shared. She looked at her biological father and wished that she could have known him if only briefly. Then she almost laughed out loud at herself. She was getting all mushy here. Something she never did. She glanced up at Doug. It was his fault, she was certain.

"You're one of them," Doug said and nodded to the portrait. "But you're also the same woman who wore overalls and carried a toolbox that I first met. Don't ever forget that, Eddi. You're still you and there was never anything wrong with that."

She kissed his cheek. "Thank you for being you."

Before he could say anything else, she tugged him toward the foyer where guests were already arriving. This was her big night and she needed Doug right beside her.

THE EVENT PROCEEDED without incident. Doug felt immensely grateful for that. Though there had been no indication whatsoever that Eddi was in any danger, he couldn't shake the nagging little worry that hovered at the back of his mind. The feeling had gotten stronger in the last twenty-four hours. He waffled with the idea that it had more to do with their almost sex last night than anything else, but he wasn't sure.

Not completely.

The only thing he was certain about was that he was helpless on too many levels where Eddi was concerned. She made him ache to finish the job he'd started last night. But he refused to go there. He would not allow things to progress that far. He'd tossed and turned in bed last night and told himself over and over it was to protect her...to allow her to share that once-in-a-lifetime moment with her future mate. But that wasn't entirely true. It was to protect him as well. He was certain he would never be able to walk away with his heart intact if he made love to her...really made love to her. So, once again he had to admit that he wasn't quite as honorable as he wanted her to think. He was simply afraid.

It wasn't that he feared commitment, or love. She didn't know who he really was and to pursue a relationship without clearing that up would be wrong. And he definitely feared revealing his true identity. He'd worked too hard to separate himself from that life. He could trust Eddi to keep his secret, that was a given. But would she forgive him for keeping it in the first place? Especially after last night?

He couldn't focus on that and do his job and right now Eddi's safety was far more important than anything else. When the time was right he would tell her everything and then they could go from there. Assuming she was still interested.

The CEO, members of the board of directors and the other prominent guests had graciously welcomed Eddi into their midst. She—Doug smiled as he watched her—had pulled off the whole refined-elegance act without a glitch. She wanted to give him credit for making it happen, but that wasn't the case. Eddi was naturally gracious and beautiful. What little he'd taught her would have been nothing without her innate charm.

Thurston had showered Eddi with attention all evening. Something about the man made Doug suspect. The attorney had been on the D'Martine payroll for more than thirty years and that had to account for something. But still...

There was just something about him that didn't sit

right with Doug. He was certain that Thurston had secretly spoken negatively regarding Eddi to the board members. It had been fairly obvious the day they'd first gathered to meet the new heir to the D'Martine empire. But Thurston had managed to wiggle out of the hot seat.

But Doug would be watching him.

Very carefully.

"Madam."

Eddi looked up from her conversation with one of her grandmother's hoity-toity friends and was relieved to see James. "Excuse me, Mrs. Deermont," she said sweetly and then quickly ushered the butler out of earshot of the woman. "Thank God you came along, James. I thought the woman was going to talk my ear off."

James smiled that kindly expression that made Eddi feel a special connection with him. He knew just how she felt. He didn't have to say so, she could tell. He'd been extra nice to her from the beginning.

"Madam, there's someone here who would like to speak with you privately. She says it's of the utmost importance."

A frown tightened Eddi's forehead. "Do I know her?"

"I don't think so, madam," James said thoughtfully. "She is a reporter from the *Boston Telegraph*." He leaned slightly nearer. "I'm not sure it's a good idea."

Eddi nodded. "Point her out to me and I'll talk to her, but I won't leave the room."

James inclined his head toward a well-dressed

young woman lingering near the double doors leading from the room. "Good idea, madam."

"And, James." Eddi stalled him when he would have went about his business. "Stop calling me madam."

"As you wish, madam."

Eddi had to stifle a laugh. James was too much. Firming her resolve, Eddi cantered over to the door and said, "Hello, I'm Eddi Harper."

Anticipation lit in the other woman's eyes. "Oh, yes, Miss Harper, I'm so glad you've agreed to speak with me. I'm Kathi Gaines from the *Boston Telegraph*." She grabbed Eddi's hand and shook it enthusiastically. "This is really a big story."

Eddi drew her hand back as soon as the woman released it. "We'll need to talk right here," she advised. "What would you like to know? I think the press release pretty much covered everything."

"Oh, no, Miss Harper," Kathi rushed to explain. "This isn't about you. It's about the gentleman you were seen with last night at the Atlantic Connection. The one who escorted you tonight."

"Doug?" Eddi's frown deepened.

The other woman nodded. "He dropped out of the social scene about five years ago. Everyone on the planet has been dying to know what happened to him."

Eddi just didn't get it. "Doug Cooper? You're sure we're talking about the same man?"

"Cooper-Smith," the woman corrected knowingly. "Douglas Cooper-Smith. Of the Boston Cooper-Smiths. The last American royal family. That's what they've been called for years. Surely you've heard of them.''

The woman's tone had turned downright condescending. Numbly, Eddi shook her head. ''No,'' she admitted. ''I've never heard of them.''

Kathi Gaines laughed at her and Eddi felt like the fool she obviously was.

''Well, let me tell you, honey, your friend Doug is probably the most eligible bachelor in the world. His family is definitely the richest and he's the only one left of the clan who isn't married. For five years no one in his family would say a word about his whereabouts.'' She lifted her palms upward in disbelief. ''And what do you know? I get sent here to uncover the scoop on you and I find him.'' She gave Eddi one of those woman-to-woman looks that was generally reserved for close friends. ''This story is going to make my career.''

The woman asked a dozen questions before she realized that Eddi wasn't going to respond. She couldn't speak…couldn't move. She felt paralyzed by the reality of her own stupidity. It wasn't until Doug's gaze collided with hers that Eddi experienced the overwhelming urge to run. He read her distress and started in her direction.

As Eddi darted toward the door she heard Kathi Gaines call out to Doug, ''Mr. Cooper-Smith, where have you been all this time? The world is waiting!''

Eddi had raced down the foyer and out the front door before Doug caught up with her.

''Wait! Let me explain.'' He had her by the arm and turned around before she could escape down the steps.

"I don't want to talk to you." Tears brimmed behind her lashes. He'd lied to her. Told her he knew just how she felt. Pretended to sympathize with her completely and all along he'd been one of them.

"Please, Eddi," he pleaded. He looked so sincere, so caring. But she'd seen those emotions before and still he'd deceived her.

She shook her head. There was a terrible pain in her chest, one she'd never suffered before. "I trusted you," she choked out.

His fingers tightened on her forearms. "I didn't want you to find out like this, but the right time just didn't come along. You have to believe that I wasn't trying to hurt you or deceive you. I just—"

She looked square into those blue eyes of his and saw the pain, knew he was telling the truth, but her own hurt was too consuming at the moment for her to think rationally. "You let me make a fool of myself." Her voice warbled and she tried desperately to get a hold on her emotions so she could say the rest. "I thought…" She couldn't do it. Couldn't tell him how far she'd fallen for a man who wasn't who he said he was…wasn't what he pretended to be. He'd played a role—the one required by his job. That realization stabbed deep into her heart.

"I was wrong. I should have told you. But at first…" He exhaled a mighty breath. "It didn't matter. This was an assignment. It wasn't personal. There was no reason to tell you. But then—"

Fury whipped through her. She didn't want to hear him say how he'd grown attached to her in a "friendly" sort of way. "Forget it, Doug. I don't want to hear it. I was a fool, okay? You didn't screw up. I did.''

She tried to wrench free of his hold but he was too strong for her. "We're going back inside, Eddi," he told her firmly. "I know there's more that needs to be said, but right now keeping you safe is my top priority.''

"Fine.'' She jerked at his hold and this time he released her. He followed her inside, but she refused to even glance back at him.

When Eddi had rejoined the party she couldn't help one damn backward glimpse. Doug and Ms. Gaines were in heated discussion. Eddi swiped at a tear that escaped her brutal hold. Everything she'd thought she knew about Doug was wrong. She didn't even know him at all.

"Madam.''

Eddi looked up to find James once more at her side. "If you don't stop calling me madam, I swear I'm going to scream," she muttered in exasperation.

"Sorry, ma—Miss Harper.'' He made a small sound in his throat, as if it went against his nature to call her anything but madam. "There's a call for you. You may take it in the library.''

A new kind of emotion soared. Maybe it was her mom or dad. God, how she'd love to hear their voices right now. "Thanks, James.''

When Eddi left the room, Doug ended his conversation with the reporter and followed. Eddi didn't so much as acknowledge his presence. When he'd checked the library and stood waiting near the door for her to do whatever it was she came there to do, she shot him a withering look and commanded,

"Wait outside and close the door. This conversation—" she pointed to the phone "—is private."

Doug obliged, but he definitely didn't like it.

Too bad, she mused.

When the doors were closed behind him, she snatched up the receiver and said a hollow hello.

"Eddi, is that you, dear? Your momma told us about the big gala tonight. How's it going? We're all rooting for you!"

Irene. Though it wasn't her parents, Eddi felt immensely relieved to hear the familiar voice. "Yes, ma'am, it's me. Everything's…just fine." Renewed tears rushed to fill her eyes.

"What's wrong?"

The voice on the other end of the line had gone on alert. Ms. Irene had always been able to tell the instant anything wasn't as it should be. Eddi was certain she must be psychic. Case in point, calling at this precise moment.

"It's Doug," Eddi admitted, the tears she'd been holding back breaking loose now. "We…he's not who I thought he was."

A sharply indrawn breath echoed on the other end of the line. "Are you all right, dear?"

Eddi shook her head then realized Irene, of course, couldn't see her. "No. I think I'm in love with him." Oh, Lord, what an idiot she was. "And I don't even know him."

"You just stay calm, young lady. We'll take care of everything."

A succinct click told Eddi that Irene had ended the call. She stared for a moment at the receiver trying to comprehend what that last statement meant. And then she knew.

"Oh no," Eddi murmured.

As she'd wallowed in her self-pity she'd unknowingly unleashed a force to be reckoned with—the Club.

She had to warn Doug. Though he'd misled her and allowed her to make a complete fool of herself, she couldn't let him be blindsided.

A gleeful smile slid across her lips.

Or could she?

"WE HAVE TO STRIKE NOW!"

Joe was about sick and tired of being bossed around. He had a plan in motion already. He didn't need his "partner" telling him what to do.

"I'm on it," he assured the nervous man on the other end of the line.

"I don't find that statement reassuring in the least," his partner said in that haughty tone he loved to take with those he considered lesser life-forms.

"Well, that's your problem," Joe growled. He'd had enough of this. "I'm doing things my way this time. So just keep your mouth shut and stay out of the way. By this time tomorrow she'll be right here with me waiting to see if her grandmamma loves her more than she does her money."

"You just make sure she stays alive," his partner warned. "She'll be worthless to us if she's dead."

Joe snickered in spite of his best efforts not to. The only one in this little venture who wasn't going to end up dead was him.

But his partner didn't need to know that yet.

Chapter Thirteen

Eddi sat very still on the edge of her bed when the soft rap came at her bedroom door. She did not want to see Doug or talk to him. She wanted to be left alone. She needed to think. She exhaled a heavy breath. If only her mom and dad were here. They always knew the right thing to do. Eddi just didn't have any experience where this kind of thing was concerned.

Maybe it was her fault. She closed her eyes and shook her head. No. It wasn't her fault. All her life the one thing that had mattered most to her was truth. Not only had her parents kept this huge, life-altering secret from her, but now the man she had fallen for was keeping secrets of his own. How could that possibly be right? How could he have been so intimate with her knowing that he was keeping who he really was a secret? Hurt and humiliation filled her all over again. Hurt that he'd hidden the truth from her and humiliation that she'd been too naive to notice. Then, of course, there were all the little remarks she'd made about not knowing how to act like one of "them" and that she was a "real" person. Doug must think her just awful. After all, he was one of "them."

"Eddi?"

The voice on the other side of her closed door belonged to her grandmother Solange, not Doug as she'd worried. Eddi sat up a little straighter. She didn't want to talk about her troubles with a stranger. She chewed her lower lip and considered that this was her grandmother and that she had grown very fond of her in the past few days. But...

"Eddi, may I come in?"

What the heck? Eddi pushed up from the bed and trudged to the door. Pity parties were a lot more fun when there was someone else to vent your complaints with. She started to open the door, but hesitated.

"Are you alone?" she asked, suddenly certain Doug was out there, too. He wanted to explain, but she didn't want to hear. The way she was feeling right now, if she had to talk to him, she'd only tell him to beware of the Club. No telling what they had on their minds. Of course they were in Meadowbrook, a long way from Martha's Vineyard. A knot tightened in Eddi's tummy. She, of all people, knew that geography would not stop those ladies. Maybe she'd better call back and let Ms. Irene know that she was okay. She'd been a little overset when they spoke earlier. If she really faced facts, this predicament was as much her own fault as Doug's. She was an adult, not a child. He'd tried to keep things platonic. She was the one who'd pushed.

"Yes, dear, it's only me."

Exhaling a heavy sigh, Eddi opened the door and

allowed her grandmother inside, then quickly closed it without even a glance across the hall.

"I'd like you to tell me what happened tonight," Solange insisted without preamble.

Eddi motioned to the sitting area. "Have a seat— I mean, please, make yourself comfortable." She'd never learn all these niceties.

Her grandmother smiled. "The only person you have to be with me, Eddi, is yourself."

Relief slid through Eddi and she relaxed just a little. "Thanks."

When they were both seated, Solange asked again, "I'd like to know what's going on with you and Doug and that awful reporter James threw out."

Eddi perked up. "James threw her out?" Now, there was something she'd like to have seen.

Solange nodded. "I have no idea how she got an invitation, but Doug informed James of the incident and action was immediately taken."

Eddi's spirits drooped once more. So, it had been Doug who'd seen to the woman's dismissal. She should have known. "No real harm was done," she assured her grandmother. No use letting her worry. The only hurt was to Eddi's feelings and even that was partly her own fault. The clues had been there, she just hadn't picked up on them. And, really, if Doug wanted to keep his past a secret, who was she to hold it against him? It wasn't as if they were dating or anything. Last night's culminating peak zoomed to the front of her thoughts.

No, they weren't dating, they'd just had almost sex. She sighed. Who was she kidding? They'd shared something beautiful. Something he'd done entirely for her, at her insistence. He hadn't pursued intimacy, she reminded herself. She had. This was her fault. But that still didn't make his holding out on her right. She'd told him everything...and still he'd kept his secrets. She was sick to death of secrets.

Solange took Eddi's hand and smiled sympathetically. "Doug told me everything." One finely arched eyebrow lifted above the others. "I was quite surprised myself, I must admit. I actually know his mother and father. A fine family."

"Did he tell you why he lied to me?" Eddi's hackles rose at the idea that her grandmother seemed to be taking up for him. She chastised herself for being so childish. She just needed to go to bed and put this behind her. Thinking clearly would be a lot easier in the morning.

Solange did the sighing this time. "No. He didn't say why he'd chosen to disassociate himself with the family name. He loves his family and stays in close contact. He simply chose some time ago to no longer be a part of the limelight." She thought for a moment, then added, "But, I believe Doug is a fine young man. He must have a good reason."

Eddi felt just a smidgen contrite. Her grandmother was most likely right. Doug was not the kind of guy who did something this big on a whim. She was just hurt that he hadn't felt close enough to her to share his true feelings. She'd certainly spilled her guts. Humiliation welled inside her all over again.

"I guess you're right," she admitted to her grandmother.

Solange squeezed her hand affectionately. "But

you're still hurt because you care very deeply for him.''

Startled, Eddi lifted her gaze to her grandmother's. "How did you know that?" Surely Doug hadn't figured out just how stupid she'd been and…

Solange smiled. "Oh, my dear, it's very clear to me exactly how you feel. No one had to say a word. I was a bit concerned when I first noticed the way the two of you look at each other, but then I discovered what a fine man Doug was and I knew that all was as it should be. I want you to be happy, that's my only wish."

A frown tugged at Eddi's face. This was all too confusing. "I thought you wanted me to oversee your company." Wasn't that the whole point? Why she was here? Why had she signed all those papers? God, she wasn't sure she could ever be happy heading a huge company. She was just Eddi the plumber. She was no jewelry designer. Attending fancy parties just wasn't who she was. And Doug, though Eddi knew he was attracted to her, she wasn't at all sure he felt anything even vaguely familiar to what she felt.

"Of course I want you to be a part of D'Martine Exports, but that will only be a small portion of your life," Solange assured her. "I want you to be happy. To enjoy your heritage. Travel. Get married, have a family. Do whatever it is that you desire."

This was the moment of truth. Eddi couldn't whine about others not being completely honest if she wasn't herself. "All I want is to be with my family. My *whole* family." She wanted her grandmother to know that she meant her as well. "I appreciate all that you've done for me, but I don't have to travel around the world to find happiness.'' She thought about Doug then and how he made her feel. She thought about how much she loved her parents and how good they'd been to her and how much she cared for the wonderful folks in Meadowbrook. Then she thought about the woman who sat beside her and she said, ''I'm already happy. I just have to fine-tune a few things.'' That was true even of her relationship with Doug, she realized. Maybe all they were ever intended to be was friends. She had to face that sad fact. She was, after all, cursed, she reminded herself morosely.

Solange hugged her, then drew back and looked into her eyes. ''You are so beautiful, Eddi. Having you here has meant more to me than you will ever know. But I understand how much you love your parents. They'll be here by noon tomorrow. I'm sending my plane for them. We'll all have a nice visit before you go back home to Meadowbrook.''

Surprise stole through Eddi all over again. ''I can go home?'' She hadn't meant to sound so hopeful. The last thing she wanted to do was hurt her grandmother's feelings.

Solange nodded. ''When you're ready and you'll be able to come back here anytime you wish. I'll expect a call every day, of course.''

Eddi nodded enthusiastically. ''And you can come and visit me, too.'' She could definitely see her grandmother joining the Club's weekly poker game, if she were ever to get over her fear of the outdoors. A little Remedy might do her a great deal of good. It certainly kept Irene, Ella, and the Caruthers twins perky. Her grandmother couldn't hide out in this big old house forever.

Solange looked a little startled, but quickly composed herself. "We'll see," she hedged, then stood. "For now, I'm calling it a night. I'm sure you have things to discuss with Doug before turning in."

Eddi started to argue with her, but followed her to the door instead. "Good night, Grandmother." She had no intention of talking to Doug tonight.

"You know—" Solange hesitated in the doorway "—we never know what tomorrow holds. When you grow older you'll realize how many regrets were avoidable if you'd only pushed aside your pride." With that said she left.

Eddi knew she was talking about the regrets she had where her son was concerned. But she was also talking about Eddi and the mistake she might be about to make by not allowing Doug to have his say.

Well, she'd professed truth and loyalty her whole life. It was time to put her money where her mouth was and give the man she cared about the opportunity to explain. Acting before she could change her mind, Eddi marched straight across the hall and knocked on his door.

She found herself holding her breath as she waited. Was he even in there? Maybe he was in the shower? She leaned closer and listened. Silence. Just as she lifted her hand to knock again, the door opened. Her gaze instantly collided with his and her heart foolishly skipped a beat.

"Is everything all right?" he asked quietly, too quietly.

Eddi wanted to answer, she truly did. But she could

only look at him for a moment. His elegant black jacket was gone. The white dress shirt was partially unbuttoned and the tie had been discarded. But the shoulder holster and weapon she'd grown oddly accustomed to were there, lying against his chest. Barely stopping her wayward thoughts, she just did resist the urge to reach out and touch him. She wanted to touch him…to do for him what he'd done for her last night. She tensed. Reality check! She was supposed to be mad at him. And the only thing in their mutual future was friendship—if that.

"I just had a talk with my grandmother," she informed him.

He nodded. "I know." He opened the door a little wider and gestured toward the monitor on his dresser. "I keep a watch on your door."

Her eyes went wide and then she pushed past him. "What else have you been watching?" She strode over to the monitor and stared at the image of her open bedroom door. Then the screen changed and she was looking at the inside of her room. Her mouth dropped open in disbelief.

"It's not what you think," he hastened to assure her, but his statement did little to slow the fury suddenly rising inside her. Not only was he a liar, he was a Peeping Tom.

"You—"

He held up both hands. "I didn't do this," he clarified before she could say more. "This was set up for your safety *before* we arrived. Yes," he said when she would have asked, "I've used the monitor to do my job, but you have my word that I used it for nothing else."

He was telling the truth. She could see it in his eyes. Besides, there was no point in arguing. Her grandmother had done this for her protection. Doug was her bodyguard. He'd only been doing his job. And she was too tired to go through any more tonight. It wasn't as if he hadn't seen all there was to see last night.

She nodded in acceptance of his explanation. "I wanted to give you the opportunity to explain." She shrugged. "I never could stay mad at anyone or hold a grudge."

Doug shoved his hands into his pockets to keep from reaching out to her. He'd made this mess himself and she was willing to give him a way out. He'd been wrong all the way around. Wrong to take advantage of their relationship and wrong to think he could get this close to her without telling her the truth.

"My father is a financial genius on Wall Street and my mother is into art. She owns several galleries." He paused a moment for her to absorb the difference between what he'd told her the other night and what really was. "I got tired of never having a moment to myself." He thought about the way the paparazzi had hounded him and all he'd lost. All he'd given up. "I started to hate my life and everything in it." There were some things he just couldn't bring himself to tell her. Not being able to persuade his fiancée to believe in him was something no man wanted to admit to. Would Eddi feel the same way? Would she ever trust him again? This time he had no one to blame but himself. He looked straight into her eyes. "I didn't even know who I was anymore. I'd lost myself." He knew that, of all people, she would understand how that felt. At least he hoped she would. ''I wanted out. A fresh start. To be just a regular guy.''

Eddi listened without interrupting, but he read the understanding in her eyes. He should have shared this with her from the beginning. He hadn't because he'd feared scaring her off from doing what she had to do and it was simply too personal. By the time they had gotten that ''personal,'' it was too late to change what he'd already done and said.

''You could have told me,'' she finally suggested. ''I would have understood.''

Why did she have to be so good-hearted? Eddi was nothing like the woman he'd thought he loved all those years ago. He'd screwed up. Let a job get personal. Broken the first rule. He had to fix this mess before it got any worse. Eddi was vulnerable right now, too easily confused. And he definitely didn't deserve her. He was far too jaded for a sweet girl like her. It would be in her best interest if he stopped this now.

''I was wrong about a lot of things,'' he confessed, forcing firmness into his voice as he said the words that were true in one respect but far from it in all others. ''I was assigned to protect you, not to seduce you. I lost my focus, overstepped my bounds and I apologize for that. It won't happen again.''

A new kind of hurt flashed in her eyes and he knew he'd said too little too late. He'd let her fall for him, had facilitated the tumble. She'd trusted him...depended on him. He'd let her down.

''I'm glad we had this talk,'' she said too quickly. Her voice trembled and something inside him twisted at the idea that it was his fault entirely. "My parents are coming tomorrow," she added as she backed toward the door. "I should get some sleep." She blinked rapidly and he was sure he noted a suspicious brightness about her eyes.

"Eddi, I—"

She held up a hand and shook her head. "Good night, Doug." She did an about-face and rushed to her room, closing the door behind her.

Doug shifted his attention to the monitor just as she dashed into the en suite bath. There was no way he could have missed the tremble in her shoulders before she disappeared from sight. He'd hurt her again. He hadn't wanted to but it had been necessary. He dropped onto the foot of his bed and stared at the monitor. She was confused right now, she would thank him later. Falling for him had only been an instinctive reaction to the sudden changes in her life. She would realize sooner or later that what she felt wasn't anything except a desperate need to reach out to someone during a tumultuous time. He'd saved her from making a grievous error. He'd done the right thing tonight.

Funny thing was, it felt all wrong.

JOE TENSED WHEN EDDI entered the bathroom and slammed the door, then relaxed. About time. He'd waited in here all evening. He'd stayed perfectly quiet when she came back to the room after the big hoity-toity party downstairs. He'd wanted to cuss a blue streak when she hadn't come to the bathroom first thing. Then, as if it wasn't taking long enough, her grandmother had to come into the room for a little heart-to-heart talk. He made a face and resisted the urge to laugh. He'd soon know if the old woman cared as much for the girl as she pretended to.

He listened for a moment longer before making his move. Sweet little Eddi Harper sniffled and then blew her nose. He'd gathered that her bodyguard had failed to mention a few things about who he really was and now she was all torn up about it. Joe mentally shook his head. Who believed in happy endings anymore? He hoped she didn't, because there wasn't going to be one for her.

When he would have stepped from the shower, she suddenly jerked the curtain back and reached for the faucet, completely oblivious to his presence until it was too late.

She gasped.

He made his move, grabbing her and pinning one hand over her mouth before she could scream.

"Don't make a sound," he warned in a near whisper right next to her ear. He didn't want to have to use the gun in his jacket pocket just yet unless it was necessary. He'd learned the hard way that accidents could happen. He wasn't quite ready for her to have an accident...yet. And he wasn't going to discount the possibility that the monitor focused on her bedroom might have sound as well. His partner hadn't been completely sure of that part. And old Joe wasn't taking any chances.

She struggled, but her strength was no match for his. He could feel her heart fluttering like a captured bird in her chest. Joe easily dragged her across the bathroom and into the large walk-in closet. Rich folks just had everything, he mused as he kicked the closet door shut behind him, putting another insulating barrier between them and the monitor. He reached into his jacket pocket and withdrew the roll of duct tape. After ripping off a length using his mouth and one hand, he pressed it firmly over her mouth.

"That'll keep you quiet for a minute or two."

Her blue eyes were wild with fear. Just like her daddy's had been all those years ago. Funny how he remembered that. He held her wrists together and wrapped tape firmly around them, effectively locking her arms in front of her. She tried to jerk free but all he had to do was withdraw and wave his gun in her face then say, "I don't want to have to shoot you here and now." She stopped squirming on the spot. Guns always had that effect on folks. A sense of power surged through him. If she only knew just how much effect this one was going to have on her future…or lack thereof. He couldn't help a grin. It was going to have a big impact on his, too.

EDDI TRIED TO STAY calm…tried to think. She trembled when he jabbed the gun at her again. Please, God, she prayed, let Doug come looking for her.

"Climb into that laundry chute," the awful man ordered.

Confusion joined the other emotions churning inside her. What in the world was he talking about? She couldn't climb anywhere wearing this dress. She'd already kicked off her shoes, otherwise she could have used them as weapons the way she'd seen on TV.

"There!" He pointed toward a small square door in the wall about four feet up from the floor on the far side of the closet. "All the suites in this place have one. Takes you right to the basement."

Fear pumped through her all over again. She didn't want to go to the basement with this man. Why hadn't she noticed the little door before? What did this man want? When she just stood there he shoved her across the massive closet.

"Move," he ordered. He opened the small door. "I'll be right behind you." He leaned in close to her face. She shuddered. "Don't think you can run away before I get down there either. There's a big surprise waiting for you." He laughed and Eddi felt the nearly overpowering need to vomit. The tape pressed tightly over her mouth kept her from gagging openly as her stomach convulsed.

"Now." He grabbed her around the waist. Her heart thundered in her chest. The image of her father flashed through her mind and she knew instantly how he must have felt all those years ago. "Put your feet in first," the cruel man ordered. When she hesitated he stuck the barrel of the gun into her temple. "Do it," he growled.

Eddi obeyed. He released her waist and she slid downward, praying that she could somehow outrun him once she reached the basement. The idea that she might break her legs when she landed zoomed through her mind as she slid past an angle.

Then she went straight down.

There was no time to think…no time to react.

Her feet dangled in the open air.

Her chest threatened to explode with fear.

She landed in a mound of linens.

No pain. She was unhurt. Quickly she scrambled

up and out of the cart that sat beneath where the opening of the laundry chute spilled into the basement.

Her mind whirled.

She could run.

She had to run.

If she moved the cart he would land on the concrete floor. He'd be injured. She'd have a chance then.

"Hello, Eddi."

A voice stopped her.

She turned slowly to face the familiar sound.

"I've been waiting for you."

Chapter Fourteen

Doug paced the floor of his room, the monitor never out of his peripheral vision.

What was taking her so long?

A generous hot soak in the tub was one thing but this was ridiculous. She should have been out of that bathroom by now.

If he wasn't such an idiot he'd already have gone over there and banged on the door to find out why she was taking so damn long. But he just couldn't bear to look at the hurt in her eyes again. His chest constricted. Couldn't bear to have her look at him with such disappointment.

"To hell with it," he muttered as he stormed out of his room.

Whatever she thought of him had nothing to do with his job. She'd been out of his sight for too long.

He didn't even bother knocking as he barged into her room. Seconds later he knocked on the bathroom door and said, "Eddi, are you all right in there?"

He hadn't intended to sound annoyed...but...well, he was. More at himself than anyone else. He was irritated and frustrated. He wanted her to look at him again with awe and respect. He wanted her trust back. He wanted her.

Silence emanated from the other side of the door.

"Eddi?"

He twisted the knob and shoved the door inward, his pulse already beginning to race as his eyes told him what his heart suddenly knew.

Eddi was gone.

He rushed through the bathroom and into the walk-in closet just to be sure. The laundry-chute door stood open. He surveyed the room again, his gaze locking on the discarded roll of duct tape on the floor. He reached for it, his mind racing toward the only logical conclusion. He checked the monitor on his watch that picked up the signal from her tracking device. She was still in the house.

Running this time, he retraced his steps to the hallway. He took the stairs two at a time and sprinted toward the kitchen. He had to get to the basement. He didn't want to be too late. Regret sank like a boulder onto his chest.

"Is something wrong, sir?" Montgomery asked as Doug burst into the kitchen. He paused in his review of what was likely the next day's menu.

"Check all the doors and windows," Doug ordered as he hurried toward the stairs that led to the basement. "Make sure the security alarm is still set."

In the basement Doug's greatest fear was realized.

The expansive room that served as storage and a laundry area was deserted.

She was gone.

BY DAWN EVERY SQUARE inch of the house and grounds had been searched to no avail.

Doug had gone through the basement and the wine cellar, which was completely separate—including a private staircase—from the main basement that served as a laundry room and all-purpose storage area.

He'd found nothing.

Ryan Braxton had arrived on the Colby Agency's private jet to provide additional backup.

The entire household staff had been called in and questioned. Brandon Thurston had been called as well. The police were visiting the homes or hotels of every single guest on the invitation list from last night's gala. But, so far, no one knew anything about Eddi's whereabouts.

"Whoever did this knew about the monitor," Doug said. He felt sick to his stomach. He'd failed. Failed all the way around. If he just hadn't let this get personal...

"That would include most all of the household staff," Thurston put in as he paced the parlor once more. "It's time we called in another agency," he announced, halting directly in front of Solange and settling his gaze on her. "Obviously, the Colby Agency can't be relied upon."

Fury flooded Doug. "Tell us again where you went after leaving the house last night," he demanded of Thurston. He didn't like the guy and he damn sure didn't trust him.

Solange held up a hand. "The police are combing the island. There's nothing else that can be done."

Her voice sounded frail, heavy with worry. Doug knew just how she felt. Unless Eddi had been taken from the island by private boat she was still here...somewhere.

"Maybe we—"

Ryan halted his next words with an uplifted hand. "Mrs. D'Martine, may we have a word with you alone?"

Thurston huffed. "Don't be so coy, Mr. Braxton, just go ahead and say that I'm under suspicion!"

Solange looked ready to cry. Doug wanted to hit the guy, but instead he snarled, "Well, you were the one who didn't want Eddi having access to D'Martine Exports. You did secretly meet with the board to try and dissuade their cooperation."

Thurston's face turned beet red. "I did that to protect Solange," he roared. "I had no other agenda."

"Mr. Thurston," Ryan said quietly, "we're not accusing you of anything. Please, give us a moment."

"Fine. I'll be in the library if you need me," Thurston said to Solange before storming out of the parlor.

"What's on your mind?" Doug asked Ryan when the sound of the slamming door had stopped echoing in the room. Every fiber of his being feared for Eddi's safety. His brain told him that this was about money, that there would be a ransom and that she would be safe for a time. But his heart didn't want to listen because he also knew that the time would be short.

"If the tracking device had failed we would know it. If it had simply been removed by someone—"

"The only person who knew about it besides me," Doug interrupted, "is Thurston."

Silence lapsed for a long moment.

Doug wanted to kill the attorney with his bare

hands. If something happened to Eddi and he was involved...

"If it had simply been removed," Ryan continued, "we would still be picking up its final location. According to our monitoring it never left the house. We have to assume that Miss Harper didn't either."

Doug shook his head in frustration. "We've been over the house twice. She's not here. Besides, wouldn't we still be picking up the signal?" The transmission had ceased minutes after Doug had searched the basement.

Ryan considered the question for a moment. "We would." His gaze locked with Doug's. "Unless the signal is out of reach somehow."

"Underground? We've scoured the basement and the wine cellar a dozen times." The only way she could have gotten from the room without his knowledge was through the laundry chute. The door had been open and the duct tape had been on the floor. She'd been in the basement; that was definite.

Ryan turned to Solange. "Mrs. D'Martine, is there anywhere else in the house besides the basement that would prevent the signal from escaping? Do you have a large safe or security vault of any sort?"

Solange gasped. "Oh my God." Her hand went to her throat. "I'd completely forgotten about the vault."

Doug's senses went on point. This was the first he'd heard about a vault. "Where is it? How large is it?"

"In the wine cellar," she said. "There's a secret door." She shook her head then. "But you have to know the code to access the room and the combination to the vault door beyond that. No one has used it in years…not since my husband…''

"Who would have that information?" Ryan prodded.

She thought for a moment. "Only Brandon and myself."

Outrage rocketed inside Doug. "What's the code and the combination?" He had to get to the vault and find Eddi. He would deal with Thurston later. He glanced at Ryan. "Don't let Thurston out of your sight."

"Wait," Solange said. "James might know also. But no one else."

"The code and combination," Doug reminded. There was no time for anything else at the moment. Whether the lawyer or the butler was involved, the only thing he cared about at this moment was finding Eddi unharmed.

Solange clasped her face in her hands and cried, "I can't remember."

"Thurston," Ryan and Doug said simultaneously.

They burst from the parlor and headed toward the library at the same instant that the front-door bell rang.

James Montgomery paused at the door awaiting permission to open it. Doug nodded. It could be the local authorities. The D'Martine plane hadn't had time to get back with Eddi's parents yet. Doug took a second to consider the D'Martines' butler. He certainly seemed harmless. He had befriended Eddi.

When the door opened, four women barged into the entry hall, all looking a little road weary and a lot ticked off.

"You!" Ella Brown accused, stabbing a finger in Doug's direction and putting a stop to his troubling considerations.

"We have a few things to say to you, young man," Irene Marlowe added contemptuously.

Doug held up his hands. "It'll have to wait, ladies."

"What is the meaning of this?" Thurston joined the crowd, glaring from the ladies to Doug and Ryan.

One of the Caruthers twins waved an envelope. "This was on your doorstep."

The ransom note. Doug didn't have to open it. He knew. He ushered Thurston back into the library knowing Ryan would take care of the note and the newest additions to this nightmare. "Why didn't you mention the security vault?" he growled, ready to lunge for the guy's throat.

Thurston looked startled. "I didn't think it was relevant. No one knows the combination except Solange and myself." His surprise turned to worry. "At least I don't think anyone else does. It hasn't been used for years."

"Give me the combination," Doug ordered, his tone nothing short of lethal.

Thurston blinked, the emotion in his eyes, whether feigned or not, morphed into horror. "My God. I'll come with you. It'll be simpler that way."

Doug snagged him by the arm. "You do that." He gave Ryan a succinct nod as he passed him.

Montgomery was busy trying to calm the foursome who'd shown up unexpectedly. Solange stood in the doorway to her parlor looking defeated.

"Please," she said to Doug as he strode by, "find her. I can't go through this again."

Doug could only nod, speech was impossible.

He couldn't bear it either.

If anything happened to Eddi, it would be his fault. He should have been more careful...should have kept a hold on his professionalism. At that moment he realized something he'd forgotten so very long ago.

Love was all that mattered in this life. It conquered all. If his former fiancée had truly loved him the rumors circulated by the media wouldn't have taken her away from him. Eddi had been willing to give him a second chance even after he was less than honest with her. And he'd given her the brush-off. If he'd only trusted his heart...trusted Eddi, none of this would have happened because she would have been with him last night instead of alone in her room.

An open target.

EDDI SAT VERY STILL. If she moved, even breathed too deeply, he would wake up. She didn't want him to wake up. Her nose tickled with the need to sneeze. It was so dank and dusty in here. The room was like a big old bank vault. She'd visited the one at Meadowbrook Bank once when she'd had to stop a leak in the ladies' room. Ms. Mildred Peacock, the bank's vice president, had insisted on giving her the grand tour.

This place was pretty much like that except there were lots of boxes and crates and even some cabinets with drawers. Eddi imagined that valuables were stored in here. But it didn't look as if anyone had been down here for a long time. Just outside that heavy concrete door, through the secret opening in the wine cellar and up the stairs was freedom. But she couldn't get loose from her bonds without waking her captor. And even if she rendered him unconscious, would she be able to get out? There was a lever on the big concrete vault door. That probably opened it…she hoped it did.

She wondered about the tracking device. It was still in place behind her ear. But Doug hadn't come to her rescue. Maybe it didn't work inside a vault.

She blinked back the fresh wave of tears that surged, then glanced at the evil man who dozed only a few feet away. He'd bragged about how he'd held her father for ransom. How he'd accidentally shot him and lost out on the fortune that should have been his all those years ago. Eddi had cried. She hadn't meant to…hadn't wanted to give him the satisfaction, but she just hadn't been able to help herself. Though she hadn't known her father, she had wept for what he'd lost…what her mother had lost. Then she thought of the other man—a man she had grown to trust. He had tricked her just as he'd tricked her father all those years ago she felt certain. Her poor grandmother. Would she ever know that the man who'd helped take her son's life was a confidant? Fury boiled up and burned away the other, weaker emotion. She wanted to hurt this man and the other one if she got the opportunity. For the first time in her life she truly wanted to harm another human being.

Neither of them deserved to live. Together they had kidnapped and murdered her father. For money.

No longer caring if he heard her or not, she struggled against the tape binding her wrists. If she could only get free before he roused. She might never get out of here alive but neither would he.

"HURRY," Doug urged as Thurston tinkered with the dial on the outside of the vault door.

The damn thing was massive. And Eddi was in there. He knew it. Two sets of footprints marred the dust on the floor. He'd noted them the instant the wine cellar's secret door had opened. A wine rack had pulled away from the wall to reveal a flush-mounted door. A code had been entered and the door had slid open. The small area outside the vault door had obviously lain undisturbed for years except for the fresh footprints.

Sweat beaded and rolled on Thurston's forehead. "Got it," he muttered as he grabbed the lever and opened the massive door.

Relief poured through Doug.

As the door swung outward a shot echoed inside. *Gunshot.*

Doug recognized the sound.

Fear sent his heart plummeting to his feet and he shoved Thurston aside and rushed into the vault.

Eddi and a man were struggling.

Doug quickly moved up behind the man and pressed the tip of his barrel into the back of his skull. "Drop it and let her go."

The struggle ceased.

"Put the gun down," Doug ordered once more.

"I don't think I can do that," the old guy said.

Though Doug couldn't see his face, he determined that the man was at least sixty. "Let her go and we'll make this easy."

His hand visibly tightened on the sleeve of Eddi's dress. Her gaze collided with Doug's and it was all he could do to maintain his composure.

"Ain't nothing about this gonna be easy," the kidnapper warned.

"If you hurt her," Doug cautioned softly, "you're dead. Let her go and at least you'll live."

The guy abruptly pushed Eddi away and wheeled around to face Doug, the weapon leveled at his chest. "What good would that be? I ain't going back to prison."

Doug saw the desperation in the man's eyes a beat before he pointed the weapon at his own head and fired.

Eddi cried out as the man crumpled into a lifeless heap. Doug rushed to her and took her in his arms.

"It's okay now."

She clung to him, sobbing against his shirt.

"I w-was afraid you wouldn't come to rescue me," she murmured haltingly.

He kissed her forehead and smiled down at her. "It looked to me as if you were doing a fair job of rescuing yourself." Fear squeezed his heart when he thought of what could have happened while she was struggling with the bastard.

"Now."

They both wheeled around at the sound of Thurston's voice.

"I hope this clears me of suspicion," he demanded, looking sorely impatient.

"Upstairs," Doug ordered. "He had to have had a partner. Someone who gave him the combination."

Thurston flung his arms upward in frustration. "The lawyers are always the bad guys," he grumbled.

SOLANGE D'MARTINE PLACED the receiver back in its cradle and started to walk the floors of her parlor once more. "The Harpers have landed. They'll be here soon." She wrung her hands. "Dear God, what if we can't find her?"

Irene accepted the cup of coffee the butler offered. She squared her shoulders and refused to allow the tears brimming behind her lashes to fall. "Our Eddi is quite capable. She'll be back, you'll see."

Solange shook her head. Irene could only imagine how she felt, having already been through this kind of nightmare before. She loved Eddi herself and she wasn't even related to her by blood or marriage. And she knew Eddi. She would be back. Irene blinked again. She had to come back.

"We should help in the search," Ella offered, declining a cup of coffee.

Solange looked up at that. "Perhaps we should. If Doug and Brandon don't find her in the vault, perhaps we'll begin a new search party."

"May I get you anything, madam?" the butler asked abruptly of his mistress.

She looked at the man as if she'd forgotten he was in the room and shook her head.

"Very well, madam."

He hurried from the room. Irene watched him go, unnerved by his seemingly sudden need to get away.

"We have to do something now," Mattie insisted, drawing Irene back to the conversation. "We can't just sit here." She stood and joined Solange in her pacing.

"Why are they looking in the vault?" Minnie wanted to know.

Solange shook her head. "Something about it being underground. I'm not sure."

Irene stood, realization rocketing through her. "They suspect a member of the household as being the perpetrator?"

Solange shrugged. "How else would someone have gotten into her room? Certainly no one else knew about the vault. Only the family attorney, the butler and myself."

Ella narrowed her gaze. "I knew that fancy-pants lawyer was up to no good."

Mattie shook her head solemnly. "I disagree. In cases like this it's almost always the butler."

Minnie rolled her eyes. "The butler was just in here serving us coffee," she protested. "How could he...?"

Minnie's statement trailed off. They all looked at each other as the epiphany buzzed through them all at the same time.

The ladies rushed into the entry hall. The front door stood wide open and James Montgomery was running down the steps as if the devil himself was hot on his heels.

"Stop him!" Irene wailed.

The man who'd been introduced as Ryan Braxton was already moving from the library toward the open door. "What's going on, ladies?" he asked in that enigmatic voice that made her shiver in spite of present circumstances.

"Mattie was right," Irene explained as the others rushed out the front door in hot pursuit. "The butler did it."

TWO HOURS LATER, Solange, Eddi and her parents, as well as the Club, sat in the parlor while Doug related the story the butler had told to the police. He had been in on the kidnapping of Edouard D'Martine twenty-five years ago. He hadn't meant any harm to come to the young heir, he'd only wanted the money. When things went sour, he'd thanked God he hadn't got caught. At least he still had his job. His partner, Joe Calhoun, was the one to come up with this latest scheme. Montgomery hadn't wanted to go along, but Joe had blackmailed him into doing it.

Doug didn't believe that last part. He felt certain Montgomery was taking advantage of the fact that the only witness to his misdeeds was dead. That part, however, was for the authorities to determine. Ryan had turned the man over to the local police and, after the confession, had called the information in to Doug so that he could inform all those waiting at the house for some kind of explanation.

Not that any explanation would ever be good enough, but the family needed to understand why this terrible thing had happened. Doug needed to understand.

Doug longed to take Eddi back into his arms, but as soon as her parents had shown up she'd turned to them for solace. Even before that, between her grandmother D'Martine and the members of the Club, she hadn't needed Doug.

Doug leaned against a bookcase and studied her

now. He wondered if there was anything he could say or do to regain her trust. The only thing he knew for a certainty right now was that he could not imagine the rest of his life without her in it. He couldn't lose her.

Eddi wished she could read Doug's mind. She looked up and caught him staring directly at her, but he quickly looked away. He didn't even smile. Almost as if he'd been caught thinking something he shouldn't. Maybe he hoped he could get out of here soon and back to his own life. Certainly whatever he was thinking wouldn't have anything to do with her.

She closed her eyes for one long moment and relived how he'd brought out the woman in her night before last. She wished again that he'd taken what she'd offered. Maybe then...

She opened her eyes. No use in worrying about what could have been. She was lucky to be alive. Best thing to do was just to be thankful for that. She shuddered as she considered the hours she'd spent in the vault with that evil man. It was still hard for her to believe that James had been involved. He'd completely fooled her.

"There's something I have to say," Solange announced above the Club members who were still marveling over their exploits of bringing down the butler halfway between the main house and the garage.

Eddi's gaze moved to the woman she had grown to love over the past few days. She smiled. She'd been wrong. It didn't matter that she already had two grandmothers, she not only needed this one, too, she wanted her.

Solange's gaze settled on Millicent Harper's. "I

owe you an apology. It's been a long time in coming and I apologize for that as well.''

Eddi's mom shook her head. "You don't owe me anything," she protested kindly. "I loved Edouard. I know you only wanted what was best for him."

"But I was wrong," Solange countered. "If I'd been more open, perhaps things would have been different." She smiled at Eddi. "Perhaps I wouldn't have missed so much."

Millicent swiped at her eyes. "He loved you and his father very much. He spoke of you with such respect and fondness."

Solange dabbed at her own tears with a lace handkerchief. "Thank you for telling me that."

Millicent smiled. "It's only the truth."

"Enough of rehashing the past," Irene said, blotting at her damp cheeks. "You're all forgetting that today is Eddi's birthday."

Eddi's mouth dropped open in surprise. Even she had forgotten it was her birthday. She was twenty-five. Her gaze shifted to Doug and her hopes fell. She was doomed. Twenty-five and unmarried.

The curse had nailed her after all.

The Club had been right.

Each and every one of them, including Eddi, teary-eyed, they all hugged her and wished her a happy birthday. Doug was last and kept his touch brief and polite. Eddi's heart ached with renewed hurt. She just wasn't sure she would ever get over loving Doug. And doggone it she did love him.

"We brought you a birthday present," Irene announced knowingly.

"Oh, my," Ella said, looking distressed. "I'd forgotten all about that. I do hope *it's* still okay."

Irene winked. "I'm sure *it's* fine. Doug, be a dear and escort Eddi out to my car and retrieve it, won't you?"

"Yes, ma'am," he said politely and turned toward Eddi.

She had to admit that his smile was a little stiff, like his movements as he followed her from the house. Whatever the Club was up to, Eddi was pretty sure it wasn't going to work. Doug probably had the same feeling. She'd heard the whispers as they left the room. They had something plotted. She only wished that she could warn them that their master plan was doomed for failure.

Eddi was cursed and Doug had his own problems. Problems she hadn't given fair weight to.

When they reached Irene's Caddy, Eddi turned to him. "Just so you know," she said, needing to do this before whatever the Club had planned made it any tougher, "I know you didn't set out to deceive me. And you didn't take advantage of me either." She shrugged and looked away. This part was too hard to say while looking into those devastating blue eyes. "I kinda took advantage of you."

"Eddi." He moved in close, trapping her between the car and his muscular body. Every part of her reacted instantly. "I wish I could take back the wrong choices I made." He tipped her chin up where she had no alternative but to look at him. Even that mere touch sent fire sizzling through her. "But it's done. I am sorry I didn't tell you the whole truth. I hope you realize how much you mean to me."

Her heart very nearly stopped beating. "What do you mean?" She had to know exactly what he meant by that last statement. Anticipation made her heart pound back into action.

"The fact is…I'm in love with you. I'd like to make this *real*." He looked hesitant, maybe a little afraid. "That is, if you want the same thing."

A wide smile stretched across her face. "I do."

Before she could consider that she'd just said "I do," he kissed her. The hot, sweet melding of lips went on and on and Eddi knew that what her momma always said was true—actions speak louder than words. Doug was just as in love with her as she was with him. It was all right there in his kiss.

When at last they came up for air, she murmured, "We'd better see what the ladies have for me in the car." She nipped his lip with her teeth. "*It* could be most anything."

Doug drew back and peered through the window of the back seat. Surprise claimed his handsome face. "It's a man."

A man? Eddi moved away from the car and opened the back door. Her mouth gaped when she recognized the minister from her church back home leaning over the back seat.

"Preacher Lansford!" She shook him. He appeared to be sleeping. It was past nine in the morning. Surely he hadn't been asleep in the car all this time.

He roused, sat up and looked up at her. "Eddi." He smiled, then frowned. "Are we at the church already?"

No explanation of his disorientation was needed. Eddi could smell the Remedy on his breath. To her knowledge the man didn't even drink a beer much less one-hundred-proof moonshine. She shook her head, knowing full well the ladies had spiked his tea.

"What're you doing here, Preacher?" she asked, trying to figure how he could be her birthday present.

He appeared to shake off a bit of his confusion and felt around on the seat next to him until he'd located his Bible. When he had the Good Book firmly clasped in hand he scrambled out of the car and peered down at Eddi in his usual kind and authoritative manner. "Why, I've come to preside over your wedding. Ms. Irene and Ms. Ella said you were to be married today." He shot a look at Doug. "Said it was necessary, if you get my meaning."

Appalled, Eddi looked from the preacher to Doug and felt the heat of embarrassment rush all the way to the roots of her hair. "I'm sorry," was all she could think to say. And she'd thought further humiliation was impossible.

Doug took her in his arms and smiled. "Why wait? We should just go for it. I'm game if you are." His smile widened into a grin. "What do we need with a big church wedding? We're here, the preacher's here."

Was he *really* asking her to marry him? Did he *really* want to jump back into the limelight of a high-profile family? "But *marriage* is a big step. You'd never be able to stay out of the limelight in this family," she countered, so uncertain and at the same time so hopeful.

He leaned down and nuzzled her ear. "Oh, but the wedding night will make it worth the effort." He kissed the sensitive area beneath the shell of her ear. "*You* make it worth the effort."

Shivers chased each other down her spine, but she tried to think rationally. "What about a license and—"

"Oh," Preacher Lansford spoke up. "Got that right here." He opened his Bible and produced a folded document. When he opened it there was her signature as well as Doug's.

"How did they—"

"Don't question fate," Doug interrupted. His eyes told her that this was the right thing to do. And Eddi Harper always did the right thing.

She threw her arms around his neck and kissed him with all the love bursting inside her. He was right. Why question fate? She'd always believed in fairy tales anyway.

If a plumber could become an heiress anything was possible.

Epilogue

"I'm so glad this case worked out so well." Victoria Colby closed the folder on the D'Martine case. "Have you heard from Doug since he and his lovely wife left for their honeymoon?"

Ryan Braxton smiled. "He called once to let me know they'd arrived safely. I don't expect to hear from him again until they return."

Victoria smiled then, too. "Happy endings are always good."

Ryan knew what she meant. Eddi was safe and she and Doug were very happy together. The D'Martine family had been united with the Harpers. All was as it should be.

A heavy sigh from his boss told the rest of the story however. "I wish there was always a happy ending."

Again, Ryan knew precisely what she intended by the seemingly nonchalant statement. Victoria had lost her only child, a son, long ago. No body—not even a single clue—was ever found to indicate what became of him. Then her husband had been murdered. For Victoria there had been very few happy endings on a personal level.

But there could be one, to Ryan's way of thinking. Lucas Camp. It took only one meeting with the enigmatic man to know how he felt about Victoria. The events that had taken place on St. Gabriel Island were still fresh in everyone's mind. Lucas Camp would do anything for Victoria. She owned his heart. But she might never allow herself that kind of happiness for fear of losing again.

"We never know," Ryan offered. "We can only hope."

Their gazes locked and Ryan knew that she knew what he meant. Only time would tell if that knowing would change things.

Turn the page for a sneak preview of
Debra Webb's next Colby Agency *title*

CRIES IN THE NIGHT,

on sale January 2004,
in Harlequin Intrigue.

Prologue

She dreamed of the cemetery again.

A cold, steady drizzle fell in the dark October night. The full hunter's moon burst through the thick gray clouds, casting an eerie glow over the deserted graveyard. Acres of headstones protruded from the lush green grass like ugly, severely sculpted yard ornaments.

Positioned around the newest of the graves were a dozen wreaths of varying sizes and shapes, forming a sort of temporary barrier from the harsh reality that lay beyond it. The carnations of one heart-shaped arrangement drooped with the weight of the rain and the passage of seven days since their cutting.

Melany pushed between the wreaths and dropped to her knees before the freshly turned soil. Her icy fingers tightened around the wooden handle of the shovel she held. Droplets of the unseasonably cold rain trickled down her cheeks. Her clothes were soaked through, but she no longer cared.

Nothing mattered to her anymore.

She squeezed her eyes shut and tried to silence the cries inside her head. Uncertainty shuddered through her, making her hesitate. The sound of her child crying echoed in the deepest recesses of her soul. Melany's eyes opened abruptly and she jerked with renewed determination.

"I'm coming, baby," she murmured. Her heart thudded in her chest. "Mommy's coming."

She plunged the shovel into the loose, damp soil with a vengeance. The sound of the metal sliding into the soggy earth made her flinch. Gritting her teeth, she flung the scoop full of soil to the side, then sank her shovel into the ground once more. She prayed for God's forgiveness as she worked harder, faster.

She *had* to do this.

She had to know.

The shovel struck something solid. Melany sat back on her heels, the shallow, muddy walls of the grave on either side of her. A frown etched her forehead, rivulets of water slipping down the worrisome creases. This wasn't right. How could this be right?

It couldn't be.

She tossed the shovel aside, a new surge of hot tears blurring her vision as she summoned her waning resolve. A dozen questions flitted briefly through her mind despite her newly gathered determination. Why was the grave so shallow? Why was there no vault?

Melany almost laughed at the absurdity of it. This was just a dream, she reminded herself. She would wake up at any moment to the agony of not knowing for sure.

"No," she said aloud, as if saying it out loud would make it so. "This has to be real." She lifted her face to the rain for one fleeting instant and realized that she couldn't stop now, even if it was only a dream.

She had to know.

Melany dug furiously with her hands then, pushing aside the shallow, remaining layer of earth. Her breath caught. The small, white casket felt smooth beneath her palms. All of her questions instantly flew from her mind. There was only the reality that she would soon know. A wounded moan tore from her throat as she leaned forward and pressed her cheek to the cold, slick surface. A wave of pain so overpowering she couldn't breathe for a long moment washed over her.

"Oh, baby, baby, please forgive Mommy," she mumbled between sobs. The haunting cries grew stronger inside her head, urging her on. She pushed herself up and scrubbed her face with the wet, muddy sleeve of her sweatshirt. Now, she told herself again. She had to know now.

She quickly shoved away more of the concealing mud. Her hands trembling, she released the tiny latches and lifted the small viewing lid with ease. Rain and mud splattered the pristine pink satin and lace interior during the five or so seconds it took Melany's brain to assimilate what her heart already knew.

Her daughter's coffin was empty.

Melany sat bolt upright in bed. She gulped in air, filling her starved lungs. "No!" she cried, then buried her face in her hands and forced away the last lingering remnants of the horrifying dream.

Her hair felt damp with sweat…or was it the rain? It was a dream…only a dream. Her baby was gone. A sob rose in her throat, then ripped out of her on a tide of anguish.

Her baby couldn't be dead. There had to be a mistake. The dreams…the voices…it just couldn't be.

She plowed her fingers through her sweat-dampened hair. She was losing her mind. She'd lost her baby and now she was losing her mind.

But what if she was right? She'd tried to tell them that her baby couldn't be dead. It just wasn't possible…she could feel her.

Melany blinked in the darkness of her room. Everything stilled inside her.

What if she was right?

Melany struggled from the tangled sheets and fumbled for the clothes she'd discarded a few hours ago. All she needed was a flashlight and a shovel and she would end this misery now.

Five minutes later, and armed with the necessary implements, Melany stepped out into the cold night air. She lifted her face to the steady drizzle of rain. Just like in the dream, she thought. But this was real. She took a deep, harsh breath and started toward her car.

''I'm coming, baby,'' she murmured. ''Mommy's coming.''

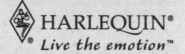

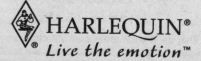

Your opinion is important to us! Please take a few moments to share your thoughts with us about your experiences with Harlequin and Silhouette books. Your comments will be very useful in ensuring that we deliver books you love to read. *Please take a few minutes to complete the questionnaire, then send it to us at the address below.*

Send your completed questionnaires to:
Harlequin/Silhouette Reader Survey, P.O. Box 9046, Buffalo, NY 14269-9046

1. As you may know, there are many different lines under the Harlequin and Silhouette brands. Each of the lines is listed below. Please check the box that most represents your reading habit for each line.

Line	Currently read this line	Do not read this line	Not sure if I read this line
Harlequin American Romance	❑	❑	❑
Harlequin Duets	❑	❑	❑
Harlequin Romance	❑	❑	❑
Harlequin Historicals	❑	❑	❑
Harlequin Superromance	❑	❑	❑
Harlequin Intrigue	❑	❑	❑
Harlequin Presents	❑	❑	❑
Harlequin Temptation	❑	❑	❑
Harlequin Blaze	❑	❑	❑
Silhouette Special Edition	❑	❑	❑
Silhouette Romance	❑	❑	❑
Silhouette Intimate Moments	❑	❑	❑
Silhouette Desire	❑	❑	❑

2. Which of the following best describes why you bought *this book?* One answer only, please.

the picture on the cover	❑	the title	❑
the author	❑	the line is one I read often	❑
part of a miniseries	❑	saw an ad in another book	❑
saw an ad in a magazine/newsletter	❑	a friend told me about it	❑
I borrowed/was given this book	❑	other: _____	❑

3. Where did you buy *this book?* One answer only, please.

at Barnes & Noble	❑	at a grocery store	❑
at Waldenbooks	❑	at a drugstore	❑
at Borders	❑	on eHarlequin.com Web site	❑
at another bookstore	❑	from another Web site	❑
at Wal-Mart	❑	Harlequin/Silhouette Reader	❑
at Target	❑	Service/through the mail	
at Kmart	❑	used books from anywhere	❑
at another department store or mass merchandiser	❑	I borrowed/was given this book	❑

4. On average, how many Harlequin and Silhouette books do you buy at one time?

I buy _____ books at one time ❑
I rarely buy a book ❑

MRQ403HAR-1A

5. How many times per month do you shop for any *Harlequin and/or Silhouette* books?
   One answer only, please.

   1 or more times a week ❑   a few times per year ❑
   1 to 3 times per month ❑   less often than once a year ❑
   1 to 2 times every 3 months ❑   never ❑

6. When you think of your ideal heroine, which *one* statement describes her the best?
   One answer only, please.

   She's a woman who is strong-willed ❑   She's a desirable woman ❑
   She's a woman who is needed by others ❑   She's a powerful woman ❑
   She's a woman who is taken care of ❑   She's a passionate woman ❑
   She's an adventurous woman ❑   She's a sensitive woman ❑

7. The following statements describe types or genres of books that you may be
   interested in reading. Pick *up to 2 types* of books that you are most interested in.

   I like to read about truly romantic relationships ❑
   I like to read stories that are sexy romances ❑
   I like to read romantic comedies ❑
   I like to read a romantic mystery/suspense ❑
   I like to read about romantic adventures ❑
   I like to read romance stories that involve family ❑
   I like to read about a romance in times or places that I have never seen ❑
   Other: _____ ❑

*The following questions help us to group your answers with those readers who are
similar to you. Your answers will remain confidential.*

8. Please record your year of birth below.
   19 ____

9. What is your marital status?
   single ❑   married ❑   common-law ❑   widowed ❑
   divorced/separated ❑

10. Do you have children 18 years of age or younger currently living at home?
    yes ❑   no ❑

11. Which of the following best describes your employment status?
    employed full-time or part-time ❑   homemaker ❑   student ❑
    retired ❑   unemployed ❑

12. Do you have access to the Internet from either home or work?
    yes ❑   no ❑

13. Have you ever visited eHarlequin.com?
    yes ❑   no ❑

14. What state do you live in?
    _____

15. Are you a member of Harlequin/Silhouette Reader Service?
    yes ❑   Account # _____   no ❑   MRQ403HAR-1B

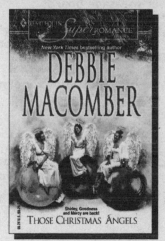

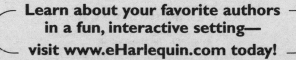

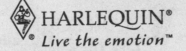

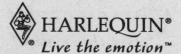